HEALERS

HEALERS

A novel

by

BROOKE REYNOLDS

Adelaide Books
New York / Lisbon
2021

HEALERS

A novel

By Brooke Reynolds

Copyright © by Brooke Reynolds

Cover design © 2021 Adelaide Books

Published by Adelaide Books, New York / Lisbon
adelaidebooks.org

Editor-in-Chief
Stevan V. Nikolic

For any information, please address Adelaide Books
at info@adelaidebooks.org

or write to:

Adelaide Books
244 Fifth Ave. Suite D27
New York, NY, 10001

ISBN: 978-1-954351-48-6

Printed in the United States of America

*“For Aaron, the only man who can openly tell me when my ideas
are terrible and can get away with it.”*

Acknowledgements

Thanks to Stevan Nikolic and everyone else at Adelaide Books for believing this jumble of words was worthy enough to be a book. Thanks to the Charlotte Writers Group for providing me with my critique group that helped influence my writing journey. To Chuck Palahniuk, whom probably will never read this, thanks for being my literary hero. Meeting you in person was such a pleasure and one of the reasons I took a little hobby and ran with it. To Richard Thomas – for providing the exercise that sparked the idea for this novel and for teaching me to put more heart into my writing. To everyone else at Litreactor – thanks for sharpening my skills and allowing my writing to evolve to create enough edge that this story needed. To Heather Seifel – for giving me pep talks and encouraging me to follow my goals during our short but fun Mexican adventure. You are an inspiration to live by as you do everything with a full heart. To the rest of my Cabarrus/Harrisburg Family – thanks to those who read my early short stories and for influencing much of the humor in this book. Having an awesome day job is what allows me to enjoy my night job of writing. To Landis Wade, thanks for reading an early version of this and providing great feedback. To my parents, who encouraged reading and writing at such a young age. Thanks to you, books are still a strong part of my life and thanks to you, my writing has improved from those early vacation journal entries that consisted of mostly horrifically drawn stick figures and me listing what animals we saw and what we ate that day. To my dogs Loki and Layla – Layla, for being the protector Malakai is and Loki for all your strange quirks that Malakai was mostly written after. To my kids Penelope and Jacob, I hope you don't find this book until you are much older. Most of all, thanks to my husband Aaron for telling me to get off Facebook and write my book. You are my muse and without your edits, I'd have a ramble of words instead of a proper story.

Chapter 1

The stifling air of the upstairs offices of Blister City Medical is foreign to my senses compared to the burning antiseptic that fills my lungs every day in the surgical suite. My hands, cracked from constant wear of powdered latex gloves, fight with the knot of the necktie that tightens like a tourniquet each time I take a breath. Beads of sweat form and creep down my spine. I check the clock. It ticks in perfect rhythm with my pounding pulse to remind me that I'm unfortunately still alive.

A slap on the shoulder from behind jolts me out of my trance. Mark, my colleague and medical school roommate gives me a thumbs up. "You got this, Scott. It's just a meeting with the board. I've survived all of mine. Try not to stare at the crotchety chick with the hair on her chin. Ugly old broad."

I bend over and scratch my knee. "Getting called out for a few office pranks is a little different than having a patient code."

"Shit happens. Just stick to the basics. The patient was critical. People die every day." He leans close to my ear and lowers his voice. "Don't make it out to be your fault."

"I'm not going to lie to save my own ass."

"I'm not asking you to. They want to believe it was just an accident, so help them out and guide them to the truth. This affects the whole hospital, not just you."

Uniform wooden doors without windows form a horseshoe. In the center sits an empty receptionist cubicle. The walls are jaundiced, like the yellowed whites of the eyes of a patient with alcohol induced cirrhosis of the liver. A door to our left creeps open and a woman pokes her head through. "Dr. Weaver, they're ready for you."

Mark waves me off. "Stick to the plan. Call me after and we'll grab a drink and a slice at Canyon Pizza and laugh about the whole thing."

I enter a small room with a mahogany table surrounded by chairs. The door closes behind me and the head of the board starts the meeting. "Thank you, Dr. Weaver, for agreeing to meet with us all today. We want to clarify that you aren't in trouble with us. We are here to support you in any way that we can. We just need to go over the sequence of events from the night in question." He motions over to the open seat at the conference table.

Six sets of eyes stare back at me from the other board members. I scan the faces and pause at an older woman with three prominent black chin hairs. I look away and take a seat.

"Whenever you're ready, Dr. Weaver."

My sweating hands fold together. Thick cotton fills my mouth and my voice cracks. "There was a mix-up in the schedule and I had picked up an extra shift." I attempt to swallow. "I had just come off a double shift. Haven't pulled those hours since my internship. I was at home attempting to sleep when I got the call."

"Uh, huh. Good. Now, one of the nurses mentioned that you seemed under the weather that night. Had you taken anything prior to being called in? Perhaps some sleeping pills?"

"No, I'm not a pill popper." I was never a fan of pills, not my drug of choice. It took me until I was 15 before I could swallow pills without gagging.

"This is just a formality. You are one of our best doctors here. We just want to clear up any confusion. Tell us what happened next? What made you choose to work on the girl with the gunshot wound to the face first? We don't fault your decision." Active hemorrhage and a half-clothed fit body seizes my attention every time. Poor thing needed a plastic surgeon, not a trauma surgeon.

My fingers dig into the back of my neck and I let out a sigh. "She seemed like a quick fix. I thought I could patch her up and get her out of the way."

"And did you understand the severity of Mr. Caldwell's injuries?"

"Absolutely."

"I see. So, you then took Mr. Caldwell to surgery. You were advised to take a break several times and still, you continued."

"It was my case. I was finishing the surgery."

"Okay. Then you insisted on removing the bullet that you knew was pressing up against the internal aorta."

"A procedure I've done before. I'm the most experienced surgeon you got and the only who was in the building."

"Yes, we don't doubt your expertise. I think that is something we all agree on. But you insisted on proceeding even after you were warned of the patient's anesthetic risk? That's a careless mistake you are not known for."

Sweat pools down my back, soaking through my shirt. I choke down vomit as it rises up my throat. "Look, I was exhausted. I wasn't supposed to be working so I had a glass or two of wine. Okay, a bottle or two, to help me fall asleep. I thought I was off for the night."

Silence falls across the room. Finally, the president of the board speaks up. "Dr Weaver, are you sure you don't want to amend that previous statement?"

I shake my head.

"If the family decides to fight this, you are looking at a suspension on your license at a minimum. You could even have your license revoked."

I bow my head, knowing what comes next. "I accept full responsibility for my actions."

"Dr. Weaver, in that case, we're placing you on indefinite probation until we can see where the family of Mr. Caldwell is going to go with this. Hopefully, this will give you time to get things sorted out."

I sit alone in my empty apartment with a bottle of vodka pressed up against my lips. I'm surrounded by bare walls and a few scattered boxes that I never bothered to unpack two years ago when I moved into this place. My ex used to say my decorating style was depressing. I spend most of my time at work so what does it matter. A chuckle rises up. Guess I will be spending more time here at home from now on. An indefinite suspension without pay because of a few drinks. Well, if the board could see me now, I'd show them what a few too many drinks really looks like. I tip the bottle back and down the last ounce.

Silence engulfs me and leaves me alone with my thoughts. I still have over three hundred thousand dollars in medical school bills plus rent for these four walls to hide my shame. I'll need to start looking for a new job. There hasn't been a day in my life since I was 15 years old where I didn't have a job, usually more than one. I didn't come from money so I worked my way through school. Work was always my purpose. What job is a trauma surgeon even qualified for besides surgery? Answer? Nothing. Minimum wage pizza delivery is my future now. With some luck, maybe a low-level management position at Target.

I pick up my phone and start scrolling through the contacts. It buzzes and I almost drop it. It's Mark, but I don't answer. Third missed call from him. We were supposed to meet at Canyon pizza after. I switch my phone to airplane mode because I want to be left alone. Thoughts of Kevin Caldwell flood my mind. His wife is probably at home sobbing, hugging his pillow that still smells like him. I'll bet she told the kids by now that their Daddy is in heaven. Or maybe she hasn't stomached enough strength to do that yet.

I toss the empty vodka bottle in the air and attempt to catch it. It clinks to the floor near my feet. Can't even catch a damn bottle. I pick it up and chuck it at the wall, decorating the floor.

I stand and stumble over to the kitchen for another bottle. I ask it if things are going to be alright. The guy on the bottle shrugs and says, "Maybe?" No work to worry about tomorrow so I crack the seal and take a long swig. The best home remedy for dealing with your problems is alcohol induced amnesia. People mix their vodka with cranberry juice. I mix mine with poor life decisions.

With bottle in hand, I wander back to the living room. I dig through one of the unpacked boxes and find an old photo album. It's filled with graduation photographs of my best friend and I, folded at the corners. Large toothy grins stare at me, back when we had our whole lives ahead of us. Before the late shifts. Before missing my ex's kid's award ceremony, school play, softball game, and swim meet. Before Mark met the nurse and got caught in the storage closet. Before his wife found out and threw him out. So many befores. What a shmuck. If only I knew then how much of a waste it all was: four years undergrad, four of med school, a yearlong general internship, a yearlong surgical internship, and a three-year surgical residency.

I set my drink down and drag my feet to my bedroom, leaving a trail in the carpet behind me. The room tilts with each step. I navigate the room like a pinball, bouncing from wall to wall until I slam into the bed. I stumble and drop to my knees. My hand reaches underneath the bed, fumbling around until it meets cold metal.

The black of the gunmetal on my 38-special pistol revolver shines. It was bought for protection when I moved to this side of the neighborhood, but it won't save me now. Bullets in place confirm it's loaded. I flip the safety off and the room appears darker, like a shadow hovering over the single window of the bedroom. My cold heart should feel something but my eyes burn dry. I killed a man and lost my job. I'm going to lose my license. My only decision to make is where to point the barrel, in my mouth or at my temple.

If I can force myself to feel something then it will mean that I'm not broken. My colleagues call it passion fatigue. I call it not giving a fuck anymore. Nothing I do matters and I can't help anyone. Save one, and three more die. Save another life, only for them to overdose later. Everyone dies. Some are just better at it than others. That Caldwell fellow would have died anyway. I don't even know if he deserved to live. Then again, knowing my luck, he was a saint, one of those genuinely good guys and I killed him. But I have a choice. I don't have to live to face the consequences. I'm an embarrassment that no one will miss.

Another shadow floats by my window, entering the room. It's waiting for me to make a decision. The barrel enters my mouth and my teeth bite down. I gag and pull out. That was my one chance. I could leave, change my name and start a new life. Starting over is for someone much younger than me. It's time to make a move.

If I die, no more playing 'God'. I cock the gun. If I don't, then I'm Superman. I push the gun up under my chin and direct it toward the sky. No more trying to make a difference. Some kid will grow up without a father because I screwed up. I can't fix what I did, but I still have control of one thing. I get to call the shots. Not God. Not the Board. Me. I close my eyes and squeeze the trigger…

Chapter 2

There's a certain staccato to the late-night city, an electric rhythm of buzzing streetlights, beeping reverse car lights, dripping sewers and wailing sirens that all builds, like a crescendo toward a climax. I wander the streets and take it all in. The same symphony of city noise has accompanied me every night since I killed myself seven years ago. Nights in Blister City bring relief from the scorching heat, but they also offer an invitation for all the lowlifes to creep out of whatever filthy hole they dwell in to wander my streets.

A voice sings out, a cry for help that disrupts my thoughts. I check my watch, just five more minutes until my shift is up. If I keep walking, I'll make it home on time for once. But, if I heal this poor screaming bastard, then I'm working off the clock. At a salary of a hundred bucks a day with no overtime pay, I'm leaning towards letting him rot.

Another cry screams out. This one more frantic, a screech that chills my tired bones. I groan and follow the sound down a dark alleyway. Two thugs pound on a man with a priest's collar curled in a fetal position. A rib-cracking kick to the priest's chest sends my feet running straight at them cuz these morons don't care that it will take me all day to fill out a 503c, the required paperwork for killing a priest. Fists pound faces while feet smash kidneys until all who remain conscious are me and the priest, mostly.

The night shadows roll in behind us. One drifts toward me, swirling until it forms into a hand that reaches for me. I jump back and kneel by the priest. Light that pours from my hand resets bones and resolves bruises to heal the priest and not the thugs. The shadow slinks away from my light, back to its hiding spot. I point my hand in the direction it left to make sure it stays away. The thugs I leave lying face-down, passed out in the grime of unswept city streets. I lick blood from my lip while helping the priest to his feet.

"My savior," the priest manages to spit.

"I'm nobody's savior." I turn and walk away.

The stillness of the night disintegrates into the motion of the waking day. Light from the sun rising higher in the sky is split by windows from surrounding skyscrapers. It spills onto the streets.

My footsteps fall into sync with the cadence of a disheveled percussionist under the 277 overpass in downtown. The rata tat tat of sticks drumming overturned buckets sets the tempo every morning on my march home from work. This is Barry. He should have been a professional drummer with the sick beats he lays down. Fate had other plans, so now Barry plays for cash to finance his habit, and that's why I'm here.

"Ladies and gentlemen, my friend Scott Weaver in the house." Barry doesn't skip a beat as he pounds his buckets. He is lucky enough to have been my first heal, a privilege he often takes for granted. An overturned frayed ball cap covered in sweat stains lies in front of him to collect his tips. "Another night of saving our poor citizens?"

"One idiot at a time." I reach down and gather up the tips from Barry's ragged hat. I count his earnings from a night of begging. "Working on a new song?"

He switches to double-time. "I play what the streets ask. They are always whispering."

"Right." Sometimes I think too much smack made Barry a little funny in the head.

"Heal anyone tonight?"

"A priest wandered onto the bad area of Sugar Creek at the wrong time of night and got jumped by some assholes. Forced me to work past my shift."

"I am just happy to see you using your gift instead of wasting it. This was what, your second heal in seven years?"

"Third, thank you very much, and my last for a while. I don't get paid enough for this shit."

Barry nods his head but keeps on drumming. "One should not fret so much about the material things of this world. You are more than your salary."

This coming from a homeless man who lives off nothing. I finish counting the bills and stuff them in my pocket. "You usually make more than this, Barry. Slow night?"

Barry stops drumming. "The city provides what it provides. Some nights are good, some are not. We must respect the city." He averts his eyes and scratches his arm.

I give him a minute to see if he'll fess up. "Barry?"

"What?"

"Don't make me frisk your nasty ass."

He takes his finger and picks at a crack in the pavement like he's picking a scab. I sigh and begin my morning routine. I check the pockets of his tweed jacket and pat down his chest, arms, and legs. Hiding underneath his right pant leg that's splattered with mustard stains, tucked into his rank woolly sock that's eaten with holes, are a few more rolled up bills. Barry jaw hits the pavement. He forgets that this is the same hiding spot he uses every time.

I hold up the bills for him to see. "Do you want to explain this?"

"That's the emergency fund reserved for all crack related purposes."

He better be joking. "This is why you can't be trusted. Do you want to live underneath this overpass with vermin for the rest of your life?"

"Don't speak of my pets that way. The rats serve as my eyes and ears. Always trust what a rat sees for a rat sees all."

I take a ten-dollar bill and throw it back in his hat. The rest of the cash I pocket. First time I met Barry, I found him passed out from an overdose of heroin. Ten dollars is enough to feed him for the day but not enough to afford smack. Part of the cash I pocket goes into a savings so every few months Barry can go to a Methadone clinic. The rest is my taste for dealing with his ass. It's been our tradition for me to check him daily since I first healed him.

Barry sticks his hand out, palm open. "Aren't you forgetting something?"

I'm forgetting that I should just keep all the cash for myself. I fish out a joint from my back pocket. A little pot quiets the dragon. Granted, it makes Barry think he can talk to animals, but I figure he's a harmless sort of crazy. He walks over to his shopping cart and digs through his things. He pauses and smacks the side of his head with his palm before coming back over to me. He points from my hand to his joint. "I need a light."

"You're abusing the system." I take the joint and light the end with my hand before handing it back to Barry. Barry knows things. When I healed him, my light gave him some inside knowledge. The problem is, he's so high all the time that even I can't tell if what he's feeding me is bullshit or if there's some underlying truth behind it. He takes a long drag then offers me the joint. I wave it off. That's my cue to head on.

I point my finger at him. "I'll be back to check on you later. Stay out of trouble."

Barry pauses and places his hands together in prayer. "May the city be kind to you."

I shake my head and walk off. Steam billows up from the sewer grates and hisses as it spreads over the blacktop pavement. Today's going to be a hot one. My weather app shows a 35% chance of fire and brimstone.

My right shoulder burns and I reach up to feel the skin morph into a shaped feather scar. I have two other ridiculous markings just like it, one from Barry's heal and one from some random chick I healed too long ago to remember. They are meant to keep track of my progress. Three heals in seven years, that has to be enough for retirement. Doesn't seem like much but when you have eternity on your side and time means nothing, what's the rush?

I head towards my apartment, thinking I might catch a short snooze after a night out. Sitting on the outside steps is young boy with a pitcher of orange liquid and a small stack of paper cups – ones you would normally keep in a bathroom. He's wearing an old red and black basketball jersey, shorts, and a look of complete despair. I plop a seat next to him and notice the pitcher is full.

"Poor sale day, Jack?" His name might be Jack or Billy or Paco. He told me once but I never cared to remember.

He looks up and smiles. "You're late."

Every morning for the past few months I get woken up by a knock on my door with this little entrepreneur and his little pitcher of liquid. Somedays I buy and somedays I yell a colorful string of profanity at him enough to make any preacher blush. No matter the outcome, he still shows up.

"I'm late? I'm just getting home. What's our drink of choice today, Bobby?" That's probably not his name either.

"Fresh squeezed Sunny D." He grabs a cup and pours the orange drink until the cup overflows and spills all over his hand. "On sale for only $1 a cup."

"You know I can buy a whole jug of that stuff for two dollars."

"Yes, but it won't be fresh squeezed."

The little hustler is good. I'm feeling generous so I slip him a Washington and take the cup. I down it in one shot. It's sickenly sweet and makes the corner of my mouth pucker. I hand back the cup.

"Would you like another? I'll cut you a deal and give you a free refill for only $1."

I give him a little push. "Get out of here before I demand a refund."

He jumps to his feet and takes off down the street. I'm about to take the steps to my apartment when the smell of steamed meat from a nearby hot dog cart makes my stomach rumble. I haven't eaten in a while so instead I head to my favorite little corner dive; Angelina's Café. It's a lovely little establishment with nine layers of grease lining every wall. The booth seats are faded and cracked with questionable stains that I'm sure would glow under a black light. Green curtains the shade of bile cover the windows to prevent any light from livening up the place. A sticky film coats the countertops. Maybe it's maple syrup, most likely it's not. I dig the irony that someone decided to call this place angelic.

My booth in the back is open so I grab a morning paper from the stand and slide in. The paper is a prop. Old school, but I like the physical feel of it and how it leaves ink stains on fingertips, even if it makes me feel dated. My waitress is bent over, taking an order from another table and I can see her ass. With curves in all the right places and a television face, she keeps a group of loyal customers, myself included. Her hand brushes mine as she sets down a cup and fills it to the brim with black steaming liquid stimulant. She always brings the fresh pot of coffee, not that burnt half-drunk liquid tar that's been sitting on the warmer for hours, attempting to change its own chemical state.

"What'll it be, Scottie?" I hate when people call me Scottie, but I don't correct her. Not even my own mother dared to call me Scottie. But I wasn't hot for my mother, or was I? Hard to remember.

I keep my nose in the paper to avoid making eye contact. This is the game we play. "I'll take the special."

She slaps my shoulder and I cringe at her touch. "How many mornings you been coming here? We ain't got specials." She snaps her gum between her teeth. I hate when people snap their gum but the waitress is allowed to get away with it.

I fold the paper down and stare directly at her name tag that is cocked over her left tit, even though I already know her name. "Well Nancy, then just bring me whatever slop the cook back there can fry up without charring and I'll be set."

"Adam and Eve on a raft. Coming right up."

I watch that tight piece return to her station behind the counter, my eyes linger too long. I'm not usually an ass man, but she could make me change. I picture what it would be like with her. I'm not talking rose petals, candles, and clean sheets. I'm talking about up against a bathroom stall, the door scrawled in random phone numbers and black mold growing between the cracks in the tile with my hand covering her mouth to keep her from screaming.

She looks up from the counter and catches me staring. Her eyes have a puzzled look. I sink back behind my cover. It would never work with her. She's a brunette and I prefer whores.

The headlines of the Blister City Gazette are the same old boring day-after-day grind. "Threats loom in Gaza", "The President Offers a New Set of Negotiations with…" and so forth. I flip the page and see a photo of our bright, shiny new mayor. I read…

Newly elected mayor of Blister City Jeff Poplar held a press conference yesterday afternoon to discuss his proposed agenda. His priorities focused on housing and education. The mayor was quoted on housing…

"Blister City is my home. I grew up here. I want it to be the type of city we all are proud to call home. I promise to build 25,000 new homes with affordable housing being the number one priority. Too many of our valued citizens are homeless at no fault of their own and it's time we make a change.

When asked what he would use to fund his new housing development, he mentioned he intends on using whatever means necessary, even if it means dipping into his own finances.

A man with a plan. The last mayor had plans, but he liked stealing more. Even if this new guy can deliver, I can't get over his bleached blonde hair. He looks like he was in a boy band twenty years ago and those twenty years haven't been good to him. The waitress is yapping on the phone instead of serving my food, so I continue on…

Here's what the mayor had to say on education…

"Children are precious. They are our future and it's time we took care of them. I vow to raise property taxes to a level that can provide our local schools with the funding they need, giving our teachers a reasonable salary, and using any means possible to support after-school programs for our children. We live in a society where both parents are forced to work so I vow to provide a safe place for

children during after-school hours. A place where they can study and play with other children in a safe environment to keep them off the streets."

Nancy sets down my plate of poached eggs and toast with a bottle of Tabasco. She points at the paper. "Oh, that's the new mayor. I wouldn't mind letting him get a little rough with me."

I stare back at the image of a man with a plastic face and a fake smile plastered across his mug. "I guess. I mean if asshats with spray tans and bleached hair are your thing. Wouldn't you rather have a dark haired, pale skinned man of mystery?" I reach for the Tabasco, twist off the top, and shake it over the eggs.

She laughs. "You mean, like you? No."

I really knew she wasn't my type when she said 'no'. I catch her staring at my knuckles, caked in dried blood, split, and bruised. Guess I forgot to clean up after healing the priest. She reaches out and grabs my hand, pulling it closer to her. "Jeez, Scottie. Were you out fighting again?"

"Something like that." I shake her off and shove a fork full of food into my mouth. It's not the worst thing I've put in my mouth this week.

"Let me get you some ice for those hands."

She returns with a bag of ice and the check just as I finish eating. The morning crowd files in, signaling my departure. I lay down a few extra bills, grab my paper and the ice, and slip out the back door.

A wave of heat smacks me in the face as I head down the street. I take off my black leather jacket and sling it over my shoulder so just a stained gray t-shirt covers my chest. The first trash can I see, I toss the ice. As I pass the laundromat, in the glass I see someone is following me, a man pushing his bicycle. He's holding his arm that's twisted in an abnormal position while still pushing the bike. I quicken my pace to get away.

"Excuse me. Sir? Please. Wait up."

I stop and turn to face him. His bike has a cherry red frame, a white seat, and a front wheel frame that's bent into a square. He's breathing heavy and I can tell by the way he's holding his right arm that it's broken.

"It's you. Oh, man. I knew it."

I've never seen this man in my life. "Can I help you?"

He reaches up to touch me. I take a step back. "Yes, please. I just wrecked my bike when I saw you walk by." He drops to his knees and offers up his injured arm and closes his eyes. "Do your thing."

I take a full look at the guy. He's wearing jeans so tight they make my crotch ache. The cuffs of his jeans are rolled up at the bottom to expose black combat boots even though this scrawny excuse for a man has never gotten his hands dirty. He's covered in layers even though it's a hundred degrees out, a short t-shirt with some woman's face on it and a sweater over top with sleeves that are too short. Thick framed glasses sit on his bearded face. His hair is styled to look like he hasn't combed it on purpose. He's exactly the type of rich hipster from this part of town that would ride a bike. The only thing he's missing is a bowtie.

"You're mistaking me for someone else." I walk away but he gets up to follow me.

"My brother told me about you guys. The guy that healed him had the same scars on his arms. He said that you guys shoot lasers out of your hands and it heals people. Straight up super hero style."

"What happened to your brother?"

"Oh, he was riding his unicycle chasing after a food truck and fell off the curb. Scraped himself up real bad."

What a waste. "Look. You can walk, right? Your legs are fine? Hell, you may even still be able to ride that bike of yours."

"Well, yeah."

"Good. There's a hospital about two blocks west of here, Blister City Medical. They'll take good care of you."

"Aw, come on man."

I head off and finally, he gets the point and stops following me. The nerve of some of these assholes. I'm off the clock and I don't work for free.

Chapter 3

The overhead lights in my favorite nightly establishment, Mustang Jenny's, dim. The stage is dark, except for track stage lights that flash and pulse with each beat. A sultry silhouette, dressed only in a black leather bikini, reaches an arm above her head, grabbing the pole to swing and twirl her body into motion. The movement is fluid, hypnotizing me under her spell. The beat intensifies. Her hips pump and grind the brass pole. I whisper a quick thank you to her mother.

A spotlight illuminates the figure as she scales higher, twenty-two feet in the air. That pussy can climb. Her skin glistens, wet with sweat. Her thighs squeeze the pole, making me wish that was my face instead. She bends over, flipping upside-down, suspended only by the juicy thick meat of her thighs. The music stops and we all stare in silence at this redheaded goddess. She's focused. She releases the pole, stretching her arms outward like she's ready to fly. I squeeze the cold wet glass tight between my hand. The room is filled with the aroma of sweat, booze, and sex. Then, her legs loosen, and she's off, plummeting toward the ground.

She's falling too fast and that pretty face will soon meet the stage floor in a pile of hamburger meat. No safety nets to catch her. No spotters to slow the descent. My feet are weighted in concrete, too frozen to do anything but watch. The squealed friction of flesh and pole ring out. She stops, her head inches from the ground. A pool of fiery red surrounds her and for a second I think it's blood. She reaches her arms back up to grab the pole and flips her hair back. She rights herself and the bar erupts in applause. The music resumes with the drop. I throw imaginary flowers shaped like dollar bills.

I look around and notice that I'm the only patron still standing. Everyone else looks at their feet, more embarrassed by me than by being in a strip club. I sit back down and drain my whiskey ginger, the after burn stinging my nostrils. A man seated in the front reaches up to the stage waving a wad of singles in the air. The temptress of the pole bends down to collect the cash. He pulls back and stuffs it down his pants. He points at his crotch and I hear him shout over the music, "Use your mouth." He laughs while making a blowjob gesture with his hand and mouth.

I jump to my feet and come up behind him. I snag the back of his collar and yank him backward.

"Who the fuck?"

He spins to face me and I sucker punch him in the gut. He bends in half with a groan. I lean in and whisper in his ear with my teeth clenched. "Now, you are going to reach your hand down your pants and kindly give this nice lady her well-earned tip. If not, I'll do it for you and I promise I will grab more than just money."

He reaches in his crotch and lays the crumbled bills down on the stage. The stripper grabs the cash and winks at me.

I nudge the man. "Apologize."

"What's the big deal grandpa? She's just a piece of meat."

I pull him in close like we're hugging, reach down, grab ahold of his sack and squeeze. "I may be old, but at least I still have enough sense to respect women." He chokes something out like an apology. I pat smack him on the shoulder just as a bouncer makes his way over.

"Is there a problem here?"

The poorly mannered man looks like he's about to say something but only mutters a gurgle. I squeeze his shoulder to shut him up and play it off like we're old chums. "No, sir. I was just about to help my friend here over to the bar for another drink."

We head to the bar. I push him down on a bar stool and warn him to leave the dancers alone. My hand flags the bartender down to order another whiskey ginger. The song playing overhead finishes and the redhead stops her performance. The DJ breaks over the loudspeaker.

"Everyone, give it up for our newest high diving dancer of the night, Linda."

That's a strange name for a stripper. I thought for sure her name would be Charity or Destiny or something else ending in an 'i' or 'y'. She uses her real name. That's classy.

This is my Saturday night routine. A few drinks, a few looks, and if Barry's had a good week, a lap dance. There is just something about the grind of a stripper's snatch on my manhood. Even through jeans, I feel the heat radiating off from down below. It gets me off every time. But there is a line that is never crossed, a code of chivalry. Never force the girls to take bills from your crotch with their mouths. That is barbaric and I'm a gentleman.

I take my drink and find an empty booth in the far corner of the joint and sit alone. The square stage is positioned at the center of the room with poles in each of the four corners. This allows for all viewing pleasures. Two corners of topless dancers for the titty fans, one corner for full nudes, and the remaining corner for the bashful type that keep their clothes on.

A semicircle of chairs surrounds each corner of the stage. The chairs are filled with hopeful members of the 'I'm not getting any at home club', all holding wads of dough.

The next group of dancers rotate in and look even younger than the last. I'm old enough to be their father. Shit, maybe even their grandfather. I run my hand through my salt and pepper hair and scratch at the stubble protruding from the deep lines of my face. I feel so fucking old.

The DJ switches tracks and the girls trade places with the next shift. I drain my glass. The redheaded goddess takes the stage again. I want to be close to her but I stay lurking in the shadows. Her routine now is toned down, more sex and fewer circus stunts. My eyes stay locked on her hips as she grinds her naughty bits up and down the pole. What I wouldn't give to be that pole.

"Excuse me? Would you like another?"

I look up and a waitress is hovering over my booth. She's dressed in a tight t-shirt that would have fit her twenty pounds ago. With the size of her rack, I wonder if she used to strip. Before I can tell her 'always', she pops a squat across from me. I adjust my jacket and flip the collar up, making sure all areas of bare skin are covered. My new scar is healed now, but I'm not taking any chances. It's my night off, and I'd like to keep it that way.

"I've seen you in here before. You usually keep to yourself."

I'm not one for small talk. I shake the empty glass and point at it, hoping she'll get the hint and buzz off. She doesn't, so I go back to watching the on-stage show.

"Ah, got your eye on the new girl? She's a bit of a daredevil. I used to be able to move like that back in my day but I never attempted the free-fall. One of these days she's not going to catch herself." She scoops up my glass.

"Whiskey ginger. Make it a triple."

The waitress nods and heads off.

I dig a girl that lives on the edge, someone who's not afraid to take risks. Take that personality, give her curves in all the right places, a head full of lush red hair, and teach her how to work a pole and it's love at first sight for me.

The asshole from before moved on to another girl. Fine by me. He's perched on a bar stool at the main bar. His hand wanders to the poor girl's leg and yet she doesn't bat him away. Instead, she laughs at something he says and leans closer. He might get lucky after all.

A clean-cut young man in a full suit and tie approaches one of the bouncers near the stage and whispers something to him. He hands the bouncer an envelope and points at the redhead. The bouncer walks over to the redhead and they exchange a few words. She shakes her head and points at her watch. The man gestures to the envelope and drops it on the stage in front. She waves to the man and blows him a kiss. They must be setting the price for an evening alone. With the way that guy is dressed, I'd guess he can afford whatever he wants.

My waitress returns with my drink. I take a sip. It's filled with ice, weakening the sauce. I point over at the exchange I just witnessed and address my waitress. "What was that all about?"

"Boyfriend. We usually encourage partners to keep out as it loses some of the appeal if customers know the dancers aren't available. Don't get me wrong though, she'll still work other angles for tips."

My goddess is claimed for the night. This GQ man is more her type. A beauty like that doesn't need a schmuck like me. Feeling like the middle-aged failure I am, I drain my drink and bid my waitress goodnight. One of the big burly bouncers grabs me by the door and pulls me off to the side. It's an early night for me and I haven't even peed in the sink yet. What's with all the theatrics?

"Miss Linda would like a moment of your time. She will meet you outside the back entrance."

"Is she asking me out on a formal date or is it secretly you? Because if it's you, I don't pack the fudge."

He only nods his head, giving no indication of who's asking. I thank him and exit the building. Looks like the suit will be getting sloppy seconds tonight.

Chapter 4

It's been ten minutes and still, I'm leaning against a brick wall next to the overflowing dumpster at the back exit of the strip club. Bulging trash bags are stacked as high as they'll go with yesterday's trash spilling out the sides adding a sweet aroma to the choking late summer heat. The ground is littered with crumpled and torn fliers, advertising drink specials, ladies' night, and the occasional amateur night. A few stray used condoms mark the previous achievements of other lucky bastards like me.

Dancers step out to grab a quick smoke or to make a phone call, but no sign of my redhead yet. She's probably still in there giving a hummer to the suit while I stand here waiting for the same. It's hard to quantitate time when you have lost track. I could be doing something more useful like hitting up another bar or hanging out with Barry. Barry. Have to remember to check on him in the morning if someone doesn't need to check on me.

Another ten minutes and still nothing. It's 2 am. Looks like another night with me and my hand. Time for me to bounce. Just as I walk away, I hear the door behind me open.

"Hey, please wait."

I turn and am greeted by a sultry figure. The redhead is standing there in a black and pink striped tracksuit with her hair pulled back. It's all loose with strands that hang down in her eyes. The after-sex look. Most of her makeup has been wiped clean and I can see it wasn't just the act, she is stunning.

"I saw what you did in there. You know, handling that creep who wouldn't stop clawing at me. I have staff that normally takes care of the handsy ones. They'll throw you out if they catch you playing the hero again."

"I'm used to being thrown out of places." I look down at my shoes and kick at an invisible stone.

"Well, it was still nice. I could fuck them up on my own, but my boss is always like, "The customer's hands come first.""

"I can add him to the list if you want."

"No, it's fine. I mean it's not, but it's all part of the job." She shoves her hands in her pockets. Overhead, clouds roll in and cover all the stars, making her face seem to disappear. "I wanted to make sure to thank you personally," she emanates from the darkness.

"For you, anytime." I tip my invisible hat to her.

She looks around as the wind picks up. A distant rumble lets out. She rubs her arms with the sudden chill in the air. "I hate to bother you, would you mind walking me home? These streets can be a little rough this time of night."

What if we get a little rough together? No, stop it, that's terrible. I'm usually against cutting in on another man's turf, but if she's initiating then who's to blame me? I don't want to seem too eager so I play her off to see if I even have a shot. "Look, with that thunder and wind, it's about to start raining pussies and poodles out here and I don't have a car. You'll be soaked. You should go back in and ask GQ for a ride."

"GQ?"

"The suit inside with all the cash. You know, your boyfriend?"

"I asked you. Not him. Look, it's not too far. Plus, I don't mind getting a little wet. I'm still a little sweaty so it'll be a nice cooldown."

She's making it easy so I give in. Hopefully, it will end up pouring and I'll get my own private wet t-shirt contest show. "Fair enough. Lead the way." We turn and head down the street. I slow my steps, falling into her rhythm. My hands are buried deep in my jacket pockets to keep them occupied. I take the silent and mysterious approach and she counters with small talk.

"You live around here?"

I point behind us. "A few blocks up." I play her game and keep it casual. "Are you new?" *Stupid.* "I haven't seen you around before." *Also, stupid.* "Even if I was sloppy drunk, I would have remembered that stunt of yours." *Come on man, you are blowing this.*

"This is my first week. I was a gymnast when I was younger. Hence all the extra acrobatics you saw on stage."

I keep my head down like I'm looking at her sneakers but my eyes drift toward those perky breasts of hers. With each step, her thin, tight jacket brushes against her revealing two wonderfully erect nipples. She's not wearing a bra underneath that top.

We turn left. Emergency lights illuminate the path. We pass by closed storefronts, all with security gates pulled down for extra protection. A few parked cars line both sides of the street. Overhead street lamps flicker on and off and create little black miniatures of us that repeatedly bump into each other on the sidewalk in front of us. Besides the sirens and occasional car alarms going off, it's peaceful this late at night.

"So, Linda, huh?"

She nods.

"Most girls don't use their real names on stage."

"Linda is my stage name, actually. My real name is Ginger. I wanted to be unique and find a name no one would expect for a stripper."

She gets points for originality.

"And you, kind gentleman, what can I call you?"

"You can call me whatever you want. My friends used to call me Scott."

"Used to?"

"Long story."

"Okay, Scott. What do you do when you're not defending women like myself?"

"This and that. Got a few odd jobs. Most days I just find ways to pass the time. Heal a few injured souls when I feel like it, rob a homeless guy under a bridge, you know, the usual." We pass one man who seems fidgety. He mumbles and scratches himself. He looks like he's due for his next dose of his drug of choice. He's conscience so I don't let him interrupt my night.

She stops and stares up at me. "Are you some sort of a doctor?"

I rub the back of my neck and look away. "Used to be. But that was a long time ago. Another lifetime." A fat raindrop falls and smacks me on the top of my head. "We better keep moving or you're going to get your wish about getting wet and it won't be the good kind."

She laughs and we pick up the pace. At the end of the street, she points to the right. "It's just down this way a little."

The rain falls faster until there's a steady stream. I take my jacket off and cover her head while we take off running. She squeals as the rain pours, creating deep puddles that soak our feet. We pass a few townhomes until we come to hers, a pale blue two story with a white door. I keep my jacket over her head while she fumbles with her keys in the door. She hurries inside and motions for me to follow.

We stand in the entryway staring at each other in silence. My hair is plastered to my forehead. I blink back water drops as they fall into my eyes and drip off my nose onto her floor. She rushes off to leave me take in my surroundings. Hardwood flooring, matching furniture, and a faint smell of sugar cookies makes me think I walked into a showroom display instead of a house paid for in singles. She returns with two towels and hands me one. She rings out her hair and wipes her face while I dry my arms. I catch her staring at my feather scars poking out underneath my undershirt. I snatch my jacket back from her and go to slip it on when she stops me.

"Wait. Don't put that wet thing back on. I'm sure I have something of my husband's lying around that should fit you. Give me just a minute."

Husband. Damn, I swore the lady at the club said boyfriend. Lucky bastard. She steps away and I linger in the doorway. I glance around the room and step over to the fireplace in her living room. There along the mantle are pictures of children, two boys and a girl, ranging in age from small to smaller, all with fiery red hair. GQ isn't in any of the pictures. Actually, no baby daddy is. Maybe the pictures came with the frames?

She returns with an oversized hooded sweatshirt that I take from her. I pull my undershirt over top of my head and she watches. I slip the sweatshirt over top and point to the photographs. "These your kids?"

"Yep. Those three are my heart."

"Didn't peg you for a mother. No offense. I just mean with your body, I wouldn't have guessed that you had kids."

"Yeah. I actually work as a cashier during the day. But now that their father's gone, I need some extra cash. In this town, third shift jobs are limited to hookers and strippers. I figured dancing was the better option."

She comes closer. Her jacket clings in all the right places. Her nipples are more visible than before. What I wouldn't give to suck on one of those. She sees me staring but she doesn't cover herself.

I lose the battle of chicken, cough, and look away. "So, you said your husband was out of the picture? Are you divorced?"

"Widowed, actually."

She's so hot right now I'm 99% sure this will only end in her laughing at me ten minutes from now so I do the only thing a pussy would, I retreat. "Thanks for the sweatshirt. But I should bounce before I ruin this or before that nicely dressed gentleman from the club comes over to mark his territory."

"Who James? You don't need to worry about him. He's my ex who was trying to get me to sign some forms for him. You're welcome to hang out here a little longer, at least until the rain stops."

She has no idea how much I want to stay. Or maybe she does. She's blind if she can't see the bulge in my pants. It's been years since I've slept with a woman. Way too long. I don't completely understand how the whole light thing with my hands works. Only a hunch, but this ends with her in a straight jacket trying to convince doctors she has a magical light-up hoo-ha. "Rain doesn't bother me. I actually enjoy being wet. I only changed so you could see my glorious physique."

She laughs. Really hard. Maybe too hard? "When will I see you again?"

I head toward the door. Her smile and that mouth of hers, I want it on me. "I'm around. I'll find you." I reach into my pocket and pull out the only thing there, a methadone clinic brochure. I scribble my digits on it and hand it to her. "I keep this for a friend. Here are my digits just in case you need me to beat up any clingers, exs, or stalkers. Stay safe." *I must really hate my penis.* I give her one last full on creepy look, sigh, and head out the door before I lick every inch of her, including the dirty ones.

Chapter 5

I'm alone again at home with my thoughts and a cracked, blue coffee mug missing a handle that's filled with three fingers of whiskey. My one-bedroom apartment, a block down from the diner, sits on top of a 24-hour bodega, always open for all my late-night needs such as booze, grass, and Cheetos. The constant banter from below of "secret" drug deals run by a high school kingpin has dulled to a low murmur. I barely notice when I'm passed out drunk.

I'm horny as fuck from my earlier encounter with Linda/ Ginger. She was practically begging with her legs half spread. I should have just hit it and quit it instead of showing restraint. She's probably sacked up with whichever lucky bastard she's got on speed dial while I sit alone looking for my lost handle. The first time I tried to pleasure myself after becoming a healer was interesting, to say the least. Nothing like jacking off with a hand that sizzles and glows. Now anytime urge arises, I drown it with whiskey while listening to 90s grunge music.

My decorating scheme is the same in this life as the last. A yellow floral-patterned couch that used to be white is centered in the room. It smells like moth balls, mold, and feet. A perfect aroma for a couch nabbed at a steal from a back-dumpster diving deal. The empty box that my coffee maker came in serves as my coffee table. The only other furniture in the whole apartment is a single fold up chair propped in the corner, reserved for all my many house guests, and a tall multiheaded lamp with a twisted base. I haven't bought anything else because everything will break before I do. There's also a TV stand but I don't remember why since I don't have a TV.

Using cardboard boxes as furniture was a trick I picked up when I lived with Mark back in medical school. He always insisted there was no need to buy a table when there were perfectly good boxes available. Mark was five years younger than me. I took a few years off between undergrad and med school. While I thought I was saving up cash to pay for school, I was really just wasting time.

It was always my goal to practice as a soft tissue surgeon specializing in trauma. As a student, I dreamed of working in the trauma unit at Blister City Medical, the best hospital in the area. Mark, without having much direction in his life, followed me after graduation because it was easy for him. I could tell he was restless and wanted more than what Blister City Medical and this life could offer him.

As I sit and reminisce, I wonder what he's up to nowadays. I thought I would have run into him at least once in the past seven years, but then again, I'm not sure how that meeting would go. Hey buddy, remember me? You probably don't recognize me without the bullet hole in my head. Then he'd just end up running away. Mark really was a pompous prick. But he was a good friend when I needed him and we use to have fun together.

A few more gulps to drain the Maker's Mark and the room tilts and spins. I toss the bottle out of my open living room window. It falls with a crash, missing the dumpster below. I lay down and close my eyes for a minute, hoping this merry-go-round in my head will stop.

"Scott, we should get out of this town before the medical director realizes it was us who filled his office with plastic forks."

"Mark, that was you. I can stay here without worrying that I'm losing my touch by dishing out lamer and lamer pranks."

"Come on. May the 'Forks' be with you? That's classic. On a serious note, don't you want to work someplace where we'll get paid a real salary. How am I supposed to afford a new boat?"

"I'm the one who actually works around here. If you focused more time on treating patients, your numbers would be up and you could ask for a raise."

"How much do you think Ketamine goes for on the black market nowadays?"

"Not a smart idea, Mark."

"It's only dumb if you get caught. I have my own DEA license so I can regulate how much I'm ordering. And I'll switch it up, you know, sell different drugs so no one catches on. A good variety. Junkies will pay top dollar for any substance, especially if it's controlled. I could even sneak some from inventory during my graveyard shifts."

"You'll get caught. And if you take anything out of hospital stock, I'll report you myself. Stop dicking around and help me with this gunshot victim's case. I think he's slipping into DIC."

"Hit him with a big dose of Warfarin."

"Are you high? That's a terrible idea. We're prepping him for surgery. He won't have any ability to clot and will bleed out on the table if I hit him with Warfarin now."

"But it will fix the DIC. What are you afraid of, Scott? I'll do all the dirty work if you are so worried about ruining your chances of being nominated for 'Physician of the Year' again. I just need a lookout. You can distract the pharmacist so I can sneak in there and get what I need."

"No."

"I'm just saying, keep an open mind. When I'm living the good life on my yacht…"

"The patient's coding. Grab the crash cart."

"Remember, just because you grew up poor, that doesn't mean you need to stay down…"

"Mark! The patient! Grab the cart, now!"

"Relax. It's all good, the machine is still doing its beeping thing."

"Mark, get the hell out of here before someone sees you like this. I'll cover for you like I always fucking do."

Chapter 6

A pounding knock on my front door awakens me from my slumber. I roll over and hit my apartment floor with a thud. The daylight blazes through the blinds and I know the sun is going to murder me or I'm going to murder the sun, whichever comes first. I sit up and my feet drag me to the door.

On the other side is my young visitor wearing his familiar red and black basketball jersey and holding a pitcher of orange liquid. My head is throbbing and I can't deal with this annoyance this morning, so I slam the door in his face.

A minute passes before there's another knock at the door. "Not today, Jerry. It's too early."

"It's 11 am."

Damn. I haven't slept this long since the last time I passed out. Another knock. I keep quiet, hoping he'll get the point and go away.

A third knock. Clearly, he's thickheaded or something. I swing open the door again. "What?"

He holds up the pitcher. "Fresh squeezed and only $1."

"Go away." I push the door but he catches it with his foot.

"Come on, please? My supplier said my quota is down and he's collecting today. I gotta meet him at the park this evening. Just one cup?"

Desperate times on the lemonade and juice stand market. I really just want him to go away and I know that will happen faster if I pay the small man. I grab a buck and notice he's not carrying any cups today. I search the floor and spot my blue cracked mug with the missing handle. It still has a small amount of leftover liquid from last night. I dump it onto the carpet and hand over the mug. He waits as I take a small sip.

I stare him in the eyes. "I paid you, now go away."

He holds up the pitcher. "Can I interest you in a free refill for only $1?"

"No. The answer is always, no."

"Please? I'm short on my quota."

I must be his only customer. I take another swig and feel the liquid slosh around in my stomach. It makes me queasy. Part of me thinks he's just laying on the guilt, but there's a weird desperation, almost scared look about him. I hand him another single and push him away from the door so I can slam it shut.

My feet drag me toward the bathroom and I dump the rest of the vile orange liquid down the drain. I look in the mirror and rub the dried drool from my chin. Heavy bags hang underneath my eyes. I close them hoping that the jackhammer in my head will stop. My right-hand reaches up to my forehead to rub the hangover away. Forgetting my gift, I startle as I hear a choir singing. Heat penetrates my skull as light pours from my palm, silencing the pain but not before a deep rumble rises in my gut and saliva fills my mouth. I turn and spill Sunny D mixed with stale whiskey into the toilet. My nose burns as I wish I had chosen a drink that doesn't taste worse on the way back up. I cough and spit until the poison is out. My knees buckle as I catch a whiff of booze and urine. I'm not sure I want to know why the latter so I grab a quick shower.

A new envelope sits on the box that acts as my coffee table. It contains my daily allowance of $100 paid out in twenties with a small note that reads, "Time to get back to work." I have no idea how the cash gets here. Maybe I made a deal with the mob that I don't remember. I really shouldn't question 'free money'. The note and the salary are the same whether I heal someone or not. I pocket the cash and think about how many ways I'm going to avoid helping people today.

My stomach churns, threatening to bring more contents back up. I choke it back. Shit, I don't remember checking on Barry last night. I grab two joints from the silverware drawer and pocket them. I need a dose of medicine myself to calm my stomach.

The city is alive with the bustle of the day. My morning soundtrack is a mix of honking car horns, shouts from angry patrons, and the beatboxing beat of a few beggars. Cars zip by overhead as I cross through the overpass where Barry lives. I feel like I'm caught in a wind tunnel as the sound reverberates underneath. A few pigeons bob along, pecking and scratching the ground for leftover scraps. Amongst the drone of the cars, I hear a muffled drumbeat, not as loud as Barry's normal beats, but the rhythm is familiar so I follow it. It leads me out of the shade and back into the light. It's there I find him, sitting on two overturned buckets, playing the bongos.

"Really, Barry? I didn't peg you for a bongo man."

He patters away with his fingertips, rocking his wrists as he slaps the sides. "Last night my sticks were replaced with these island beauty drums. A gift from the city."

"A gift or did you steal them?" I hope he's still sober. "I leave you alone for one night and already you're causing trouble. Set those obnoxious things down and stand up. I know I'm late but we'll get this over with quickly."

"One cannot be late, just not on time." He stretches his hands out to his sides, and I pat him down. "The streets say you walked a lady home last night. A pretty one too. You need a good woman to keep you grounded."

"Hand me your shoes." Jammed in the front of the right one is a hidden extra wad of cash. I pocket the money and hand him back his shoes. "Don't read into things. It wasn't anything more than a walk home."

"A walk is never just a walk. There are only so many missed opportunities for chickens like yourself." He holds out his left hand, palm up.

I hand him ten bucks and light up a joint. "Slide that other bucket over here. I'm joining you today." The smoke fills my lungs. I exhale and hand over Barry's daily allowance.

Barry smiles and we both sit. He inhales a deep hit, and hands me the joint. I'm halfway through my inhale when he takes it back. "My medicine keeps me grounded but it will impair your ability to do your healing. I do not need the man in the sky mad at me if you leave here and try to heal a fire hydrant. Therefore, more for me and less for you." He takes another hit.

I take the joint back. "Remember who supplies your medicine. I do my part. Each night I hunt for trouble, beat up a few vandals, and spend the rest of the night passed out. Rinse and repeat." I take another deep drag, blowing the smoke from my nostrils like I know what I'm doing. My lungs burn and my eyes water as I stifle a cough, too embarrassed to seem like an amateur.

Barry folds his hands in prayer and stares up at the sky. "Forgive this man for wasting his gift."

I'm not wasting anything. There's no rush when I have all of eternity. I nudge him. "I need a change in scenery. I've been frequenting the same spots each night and there's no one left to rough up."

Barry pauses with his hand on his chin. A vessels pulses on his forehead like he's concentrating too hard. "I saw one of your old friends last night. The spikey male blonde-haired doctor one."

"Mark? How the hell do you know Mark?"

He takes another hit from the joint but doesn't offer it back to me. "Fidgety one, he is. We were business acquaintances. He supplied me with used gum back when you gave me money."

"Are you sure it was him?"

Barry nods. "One never forgets his suppliers."

"Where did you see him?"

Barry points behind him. "Stone's throw south and across the street."

The only thing off in that direction is a shady bar and a junk yard. I wouldn't be caught dead over there. Well, assuming I'm not dead already. Seems very unlikely, but Barry has a surprisingly strong sense of direction. "Near the corner of 9th and Frasier?"

He nods.

The junk yard is the same as any old junk yard. The bar, know by locals as 'The Underground', is frequented by all the filth of Blister City. Mark, being the most shallow individual I know, wouldn't dare to be seen anywhere that wasn't the latest hip scene.

I tap Barry on the forehead. "I think the drugs have left you cloudy, my man. Or, we're not talking about the same guy here."

He shrugs and finishes off the joint.

"The Underground is filled with drug dealers and junkies a like. Not Mark's scene."

Barry waves his hands in front of his face. "These eyes may be getting older, but they never tell a lie."

An argument with a crazy old ex-heroin addict is not worth my day. I stand and brush at my jeans. The pot helped settled my stomach but gave me the munchies. I'm in desperate need of some food. I reach in my back pocket and pull the extra joint out and hand it to Barry. "This is because I was late."

Barry picks up his bongos and drums away again. I head in the opposite direction, toward Angelina's Cafe for the hangover cure special. It doesn't matter what I eat, as long as it's triple fried and Nancy's working. I spend an hour or more talking with her about the weather before I head back out for my Sunday stroll.

My mind drifts back to this morning and the worried look on my Sunny D supplying little friend. I decide to go check on him since I still have the light of day on my side and time to waste. I head north in the direction of Sugar Creek Park, a small public park tucked away in the center of Blister City. It's the only park in the city and on a nice day, the most likely place to find my little friend. It has all the nice amenities of a typical city park: a small rusted playground covered in grafiti, walkways with mutant grass that pushes through the cracks of the pavement, and a baseball field with a falling down fence and used syringes covering the floor of the dugout. There's even a disc golf course on the outskirts where most of the chains are missing from the baskets. The center of the park contains a single covered pavilion. It's here I gamble with the regular crowd while I wait for the kid and the sun to dip down.

Three women who smell of moth balls with sagging tits, powered-wig style hair, thick glasses, and bent over frames sit across from me. One woman's hand, wrinkled and crooked, trembles as she spills the dice from a black cup out onto the splintered picnic table. The dice knock and smack into each other, jutting for position, until all five land with one dot pointed toward the sky.

"Yahtzee," the woman yells.

"Now Mildred, that's the third one you rolled today. I think you have some trick dice up your sleeve."

The woman hands me the cup and I scoop up the dice and shake. A popping sound rings out and no one startles. It sounds like the backfire of a car engine. I throw my three allotted rolls and come up empty. One more pop sound echoes across the park. The game continues until the sun dips down in the sky and the ladies load up in their Lincoln Town Car and head home.

I take a loop around the park, looking for the kid. The basketball court contains a fresh coat of red graffiti. A few kids, all wearing red and black jerseys, standby with a ball like they're waiting for the next game. The court is surrounded by a single layer of yellow police tape. Blue and red flashing bulbs light up the court. Just off to the side of the pool of red lays a pitcher with a small amount of orange liquid still dumping onto the ground. Men wearing uniforms carry away one small human sized trash bag. Not wanting to hear the answer but knowing I need to, I pull one of the waiting kids to the side and ask him what went down. He mumbles something about his friend being a runner and being short on his quota.

As I watch the graffiti dry, I stand and regret my stupidity. How did I not see this? Kids in Blister City don't sell Sunny D or lemonade for that matter, they move drugs. All those mornings of annoyance and I could have helped the kid out, found out who he worked for and bailed him out. Instead, I couldn't even remember the kid's name. I hate seeing the youth portrayed as the victims of our mistakes. The city is broken and I need to do something about it.

Barry's conversation jumps to the front of my mind. There's one hot spot meeting ground for all the worse drug deals. To-night, I'll check out The Underground.

Chapter 7

The stench of last week's vomit mixed with this week's vomit smacks me in the face as I enter the door of The Underground. It's right around 10 pm. The doorman makes me buy a membership for a buck; says something about keeping the other folk out, whatever that means.

The bar is a one-story shack, located in an old farm equipment store. Confederate flags hang amongst a sea of braziers draped from the ceiling. These are not the 'I'm gonna get lucky' little bras with lace trim. These are the oversized offbrand type meant for holding up old sagging tits. The banner behind the barkeep reads, "Shut Up and Drink." Tall boys of PBR, Bud Light, Miller Light, and Mickey's grenades are the drinks of choice, instead of irony. A collection of liquor with faded labels line a single shelf. My options are single, double, or triple shots of either clear or brown. A craft beer order could get me stabbed, a cocktail order might get me killed.

I find a seat at the bar and nurse my Mickey's grenade, tonight's special. The green glass is at least cold against my fingers. I twist the cap to break the seal and down a long swig of beer flavored water that should keep me sober enough. The sad patrons seated next to me are shaggy bearded, ball cap-wearing, tobacco spitting, full-on country folk. They spit their wad straight onto a floor that hasn't met a mop in a year. I keep my jacket zipped up and my head low. I don't want to attract any extra unwanted attention.

Some honky-tonk coverband sings songs that echo heartbreak, and I couldn't feel more out of place. Darts whiz by in the back and strike the wall, the floor, just about everything but the board. Two guys argue over a game of pool. The one gentleman makes a comment about calling the wrong pocket. The other makes a comment about sleeping with the wrong woman. The one slams the other onto the table but no one makes a move to break them up. The center of the table is bare from where the felt has been ripped off during previous disagreements. The band takes a break.

I take my grenade with me to the pisser. The writing on the door makes me halt. "Us". I look around and there is a similar door behind me with a different word on the door. "Them". Come to think of it, this bar has one female in it and even that is debatable.

The handle of the bathroom door has a visible film on it that would glow under a blacklight. I push through the "Us" door and the stench makes me gag. The walls are pea shit green and I'm guessing that is not the original color. Toilet paper, used rubbers, and broken glass are spread on a floor of thick grime with black mold collecting in the cracks. I unzip over the single toilet in the room that is covered in a swarm of flies. Grenade in one hand, dick in the other, I touch nothing else.

Back at the bar, there's a new guy sitting five stools down who also seems out of place. His attire is more homeless than country, with an overstretched t-shirt and pants two sizes too big and blonde hair that's stringy and plastered to his head. His eyes dart behind him to the front door and he's jumpy, like he just pounded two energy drinks. Shave five to ten years, clean him up and feed him ten Big Macs and I swear he could pass as the twin of my med school friend Mark.

The door bursts open as two big burly white guys head straight for my old friend lookalike. One gives a shove and his stomach slams into the bar. He coughs and wheezes. The pour scrawny soul waves at the barkeep, begging for help, but the barkeep shakes his head and ignores him as he continues to pass out beers.

One of the large brutes has a skull tattoo on his forearm like he's a damn pirate. He grabs the back of his victim's collar and drags him toward the front door. That poor bastard has the same look a baby bunny has when it's being carried off in the talons of a hawk; pure terror. He screams and cries and snot pours out of his nose. No one else seems to notice or they don't seem to care. This is what I've been waiting for; this kind of drama. The three gentlemen leave the bar, and I give them a head start while closing out my tab. I love the thrill of a chase.

I hit the door with both hands on the run. I think I'm making a grand exit, but forget I just left a bar where no one gives a shit. It's unusually dark for this time of night. Clouds cover the night sky and in the distance a rumble of thunder lets out. Left is the direction of downtown. Right is the direction of the projects. I head right. My feet pound the pavement at a steady jog. I pass a Family Dollar store with bars over the window. I laugh out loud at the fact that anyone gives a shit if someone robs a dollar store. Barbed wire fences separate me from train tracks and intermittent street lights guide my way. My feet continue to strike light and dark pavement, altering with each footstep.

A few murmurs, a plea for help, and I think I'm close. I turn a corner, trip on a crack, and fall hard to the ground. I roll over to see the two big guys from the bar with guns pointed at their offender. He's curled in the fetal position on the ground to protect himself, draped in shadows, as legs kick and stomp. He shakes and sobs. Some speck of light that remains in my cold heart feels sorry for the bastard.

Direct seems like the best approach, so I push myself up off the pavement and head towards them. The echo of gunshots rings out. Something strikes my shoulder and pushes me back, but I continue on. The man on the ground's body jerks like he just got hit by shock paddles in the ER. I've seen that motion one too many times. My rage takes over and I run straight into the line of fire. A bullet pops me in the center of my forehead, perfect shot, dropping me to the pavement.

A single shadow separates itself and floats in my direction like it has a mind of its own. Rather than any particular color, it is the absence of all color, but thick and billowy, like the pollution from factory exhaust pipes. The shadow whispers but I can't make out any words. A chill runs through me as it drifts closer. Every hair on my body stands fully erect. Using my last remaining strength, I place my hand on the bullet hole. Light shines from my hand. The shadow regresses and the bullet snakes its way back out. It falls to the pavement. I rub my forehead, smearing blood, and sit up. The thugs with guns look at each other wide-eyed and run off.

I make my way to the guy sprawled across the ground and realize my suspicions were true. It's Mark. I don't need confirmation by checking his wallet ID but I do for the hell of it. This should be a piece of cake. With all the hours we spent in emergency saving lives in surgery, no one deserves to be healed as much as he does.

My hand glows as it reaches his first bullet entry point. The light is dim. Then it stops. I shake my hand and try again. This time, one small spark sputters, then nothing. What the hell? Do I have to recharge this thing? Without my light, the shadow moves in. My other hand applies direct pressure to the wound. Mark moans and his chest sounds wet and crackles. It's the sound lungs make when they fill with blood. What I wouldn't give for a chest tube right now. He coughs bubbled red spit that leaks out of the corner of his mouth. I'm losing him. Pleading, swearing, straining and using all my concentration I try to force the light from my hand. Still, nothing.

The shadow shifts into a condensed shape, forming a dark spirit figure. It passes straight into my body. I wheeze and my heart feels like it's being stabbed by spears of ice. There's a flash and I see myself back in my apartment. I watch myself pick up my gun and point it under my chin. My body sways and the sound of the gun explodes. I cough and the shadow leaves my body.

I'm back in the street next to Mark. The shadow forms into a dark hand. I reach my hand up to push it away. "Get the fuck away from us."

It reaches down Mark's throat. Mark's eyes roll back into his head and his body convulses into a seizure. I place my jacket under his head and begin CPR. My arms slam down onto his chest until I feel his ribs crack beneath my weight. "Oh, no you don't. Stay with me, Mark. Stay alive, you bastard." Mark's body stills. He exhales and the shadow leaves through his mouth. I feel for a pulse. I feel…

Chapter 8

I need to get drunk, funeral drunk. The low music with a rhythm as smooth as a glassy sea surrounds and blankets me in the comfort of my favorite strip joint. I should feel relaxed but instead, I'm drowning.

Three drinks in and Mark's bloody face still hovers at the front of my memory. I picture the shadow leaving Mark's body, taking with it all the life left in him, and me sitting there unable to do a damn thing. Then, I see the kid, his little frame sprawled across the basketball court, still holding that stupid pitcher. I choke back a sob cuz I can't be seen crying in a strip club. No more early morning wakeup calls. I wash the images away by downing another whiskey ginger.

The overhead lights dim down and the music changes to a faster beat. My foot taps along. I know this song. It's the red head's song. My whiskey-induced courage guides me to her corner of the stage. The front row is occupied so I pick the scrawniest patron and force him to sit elsewhere. He attempts to protest so I give him my best junkyard dog growl until he gets the hint. I plop myself down in his seat.

She struts out onto the stage and grabs onto the pole, working it to the music. Her all black bikini has been replaced with a white ruffled lace bikini, her long red hair loose with soft curls. The spotlight dances and sparkles off her shimmering bare skin. She's suspended, legs wrapped around the pole, just about a foot off the ground. She spins around and her face lights up in a full smile when she sees me. My eyes drink her in with a locked predator stare.

The song is reaching its climax and Ginger winks at me. She scales the pole with ease, pausing at the top to grind the cold steel before flipping upside down. The music stops and she hangs, bringing her body to a standstill. I'm holding my breath even though I've seen this routine before. She exhales with her arms spread eagle. The muscles of her thighs quiver as she holds herself. Then comes the release and she soars to the ground until the squeal of her flesh against the pole brings her to a skidding halt. The crowd roars as the music drops and she flips herself upright. I need to feel her on top of me.

I find one of the bouncers and pull him aside. We exchange words and a wad of cash, enough for the full package. He tells me to wait a minute so I down the rest of my drink. Ginger exits the stage. I have a rule, never pay for sex on Mondays. But tonight, rules don't apply.

The bouncer escorts me onto the stage and places a hard, cold metal fold out chair in the center. A few extra bills, mostly singles and fives, poke out of the neck of my zipped-up jacket. The bouncer goes over the rules but they fall on deaf ears. I consider myself an old pro in the act of receiving lap dances. My hands are pinned underneath my legs so I'm not tempted to touch her. The DJ makes an announcement overhead.

"Ladies and gentlemen, give it up for Linda as she is about to make this guy's night very special."

My redhead struts back out on stage. She turns to see me and has a surprised look on her face. She parades around in front of the crowd, working the audience to gain all their attention. Her back is towards me and I stare at her tight ass, shoved into that tiny white lacy bikini, as it sways in front of my face. Her long curls bounce and dance with each step. She spins and faces me. She walks around behind the chair, her hands graze my chest and come to a rest on my shoulders. I shiver at her touch.

The lights drop and she leans in to whisper in my ear. "I was afraid I scared you off after you didn't take me up on my offer the other night. You know, you don't need to pay for my attention. I thought I made that clear."

"I was trying to be a gentleman and just walk a lady home."

She laughs. "I can tell you are not a gentleman and that's what I like about you. After this song is over, I dare you to say no to me again."

Before I have a chance to respond, the spotlight blazes on us and the music starts. She lifts her leg straight in the air, over her head. Her hand remains in contact with me the whole time. She saunters to the front of the chair and bends over, her ass directly in my face, and rocks her hips to the music, the same motion she uses on the pole. Both hands are balled into fists beneath me and I exhale to keep calm. Even in a packed house, my focus is just on her. She spins and straddles me. She leans in close and grabs each and every bill with her teeth, her lips brushing against my neck.

She takes the bills from her mouth and slides them down the front of her bra. She readjusts herself just so I can sneak a quick peak at her dark erect nipples. The music pulses loud and I can feel the vibrations of the base through my whole body. She grabs the chair behind my neck with both hands to keep her hovering above me and rocks and grinds over my crotch. She smiles. "I can make you want me."

I play it off smooth. "Honey, when you haven't been laid in as long as I have, any chick shaking their ass in front of me could give me a hard-on."

Her hand reaches back and slaps me across the face. I reach my hand up to rub my cheek. The slap was hard and I can't tell if it was too hard.

The DJ addresses the crowd. "Ladies and Gentleman, wow. That's the first time I've seen a customer slapped for not grabbing the girl."

Ginger makes a motion for the DJ to start the music back up. She continues to grind up and down, her hips roll and gyrate in perfect cadence, alternating between slow and fast thrusts. She leans in again. "You're kind of an ass, you know that?"

Her hips stop rolling and I think she is about done. Instead, she lifts one leg at a time and places them on my shoulder, straddling my face, the lace of her panties brushing up against me. I breathe in her scent. She grinds in front of me and I almost come undone. My arms shake and there's a pleading desperation in my eyes. One more pump of her hips and the music stops. The spotlight cuts down and we are left in total darkness.

She removes her legs one at a time and my face is dripping with sweat. She runs her fingers through my salt and pepper hair and drags one finger down the front of my face. Her lips brush against my ear and her breath sends shivers as it cools my face. She whispers. "Walk me home?"

I nod, unable to speak.

Ginger pulls me out of my trance with a second slap to the face, this one harder than the last. "I'll meet you out back when I get off."

She waves to the crowd and runs off stage. I stand and the audience laughs, pointing at my erection throbbing against my pants. A stage hand pushes me off stage.

"Times up, buddy. We have another shift of girls coming out and I need you off this stage." He points at the stiffness in my pants. "There's a bathroom down the stairs and to the left for you to take care of that."

I limp off the stage with my third leg and head to the restroom. The walk calms me, and I feel my pants loosen. The door pushes open and a young man with a pale face races past me into the bathroom. He smells musky as if he bathed in discount cologne.

There're three stalls and the first one, closest to the sink, contains some poor amateur who's bent over the mighty white porcelain spilling his stomach contents up as an offering. I try to ignore the guttural sounds and head to the sink. Cool water fills my cupped hands and offers refreshing relief as it splashes on to my face. A man dressed in a tuxedo hands me a towel to dry my face like I'm some high-class executive and not just some schmuck who just paid to get his jollies off. I pat the water off and stare at my sorry excuse of a reflection. Flashes of Mark with dark shadows that choke him stare back at me. The fragmented memories blink away.

Behind me, a man with bleached blonde hair and a bad tan approaches the sink. He washes his hands with soap and points to the occupied stall where the chorus of hurling stomach contents continues. "I hope that guy isn't driving home tonight."

I nod. The man accepts a towel as well as a handful of lotion. What a pansy. I take a good look at him and realize he's the guy from the paper, Mayor Jeff Poplar. He thanks the tuxedo and hands him a bill before leaving the restroom. From what I've read, the mayor was working to clean up this city. He better not be trying to shut down this joint.

The tuxedo clear his throat. He nods his head over at the tip jar and looks back at me. I shrug. All my cash was left with the stripper.

Back out on the main floor, I catch a glimpse of the mayor perched over in the VIP lounge, his obnoxious hair visible from across the room. He's surrounded on either side by two suits. The second shift girls are on stage rubbing and pumping the pole. They're tight and perky in all the right places. They must be at least ten years younger than Ginger, perhaps more. There's one girl, a blonde, who's especially lively. She spins and twirls faster than any of the other girls, her bones look like they are made of putty the way she bends and twists. She's flat chested compared to the other girls. I guess she hasn't worked up enough tips to pay for a boob enhancement yet. What she lacks in bra size, she makes up for in energy. Just watching her is a young man's game.

The mayor whispers something to one of the suits and points at the young blonde. My waitress from the other night is tending bar. I pull up a seat at the bar and order a drink.

"That was some performance you got up there on stage. That slap even looked real." She slides me a straight whiskey on the rocks; no mixer tonight.

I nod and take a sip. The mayor's suit hands off a wad of cash to the bouncer who walks over to talk with the flat chested energetic dancer.

I turn to address the waitress. "Why do you think a guy like him is hanging out here?"

"Who? The mayor? He comes here sometimes. Everyone needs their fix."

The girl with no tits smiles and walks over to the mayor. She grabs his hand and leads him to the back of the club. It looks like he's getting some high school action tonight.

Chapter 9

The scratchiness of the brick wall behind me digs into my back but the chill of a late-night breeze cools my body as I stand and wait for Ginger. The fresh air helps to sober me up and that is the last thing I need right now. Mark's death scene repeatedly flashes in front of me, with me standing on top of him with a hand that can only sputter. I stare down at my hand now and wonder if this is permanent and then realize that I don't care.

The door opens and she saunters through, her hair pulled up on her head and the same pink and black tracksuit from the last time I walked her home. She smiles and stands on her tiptoes. I flinch, waiting for my third slap of the night. Instead, she offers a small kiss on the cheek. There's a bounce in her step as we head towards her place.

She turns her head and watches me. "You know, you could have saved your money. I would have given you a dance for free the other night."

I smirk. "Wanted the whole experience, the DJ rocking a beat and a full audience laughing at me."

She laughs. We walk the next few blocks to her home in silence. The sky is clear without a single cloud. The few stars that aren't swallowed by the city lights gleam and flicker in the sky. One could say it's the perfect night for romance. I say, it's the perfect night for screwing.

Ginger jogs up her steps two at a time. With her keys in hand, she unlocks the door and swings it open. I follow her up the stairs but wait outside on her doorstep.

She sees me wait. "What is this? You aren't some kind of vampire who needs permission to enter my home are you?" She laughs.

"I don't think so?" I pause to think it over. That would make sense since I'm basically nocturnal. Who am I kidding, that's ridiculous.

She grabs my jacket. "Then get in here." She pulls me through the door, and slams it behind me. "Make yourself at home. Grab a drink or whatever. I'm going to change into something more appropriate. Try not to pussy out and run away on me."

She scampers off and I'm left alone. In the living room I stare at her row of pictures. She seems genuinely happy. This is a woman that loves her children to the point that she is willing to grind on nasty old men night after night to provide for them. I've always been a sucker for single moms.

I hear a voice from down the hall. "Okay. I'm ready. The bedroom is the second door on your right."

I open the door to find her tone body sprawled out on the bed. She's wearing a white lace thong with black trim. My eyes drift up her body and hover over her perfect, exposed tits. I usually prefer the natural look, but these beauties are just so supple and begging to be squeezed and sucked on. Her hair falls perfectly around her face. She looks heavenly. She looks beautiful.

She cocks her head. "What's wrong?"

I want to leap onto the bed and drive into her again and again until my dick is raw and chaffed. That's how much I want this. "Nothing."

She sits up. "Then come join me."

I sit on the edge of the bed with my back toward her, facing the door. "I haven't done this in a while."

"Then I'll make sure to take it easy on you."

She crawls up behind me and reaches her hands around, grabbing the zipper of my jacket, and slowly pulls it down. She removes my arms one at a time and tosses the jacket onto the floor. Her fingers work their way underneath my shirt and up my back, slipping my undershirt up over my head. She pauses. Her fingers trace over each feather scar, rising higher until they reach a small crater on my shoulder. "This looks new." Her lips kiss the tender bullet wound in my shoulder that I forgot to finish healing. Her tongue licks the edges, like an injured dog licking its wounds.

I turn my face toward her. We stare and she leans in to kiss me, her hand resting on my chin. She's tender and soft but I need more. My tongue wrestles hers and I drink her in, our teeth knocking into each other. I get off the bed and fall to my knees, grab her legs and pull her to the edge of the bed. Her legs part and I push my face in her crotch. I turn to the inside of her thighs, kiss them and nip with my teeth, teasing her. Blood pumps and fills me until I'm hard. My hands reach up and rip down her panties. I lick up the wetness between her legs with my tongue. This chick is ready to go.

I undo my pants, grab her legs, and drive into her. She lets out a gasp and takes all of me. Her hips rock to meet mine and there's urgency in both of our motions. Our pelvic bones slam into each other in an odd rhythm as we try to figure each other out. She grabs my hip to slow me down to match her pace. She moans like she's in pain but she's not telling me to stop. My hand feels warm and I see a dim light glow. I smack my hand against the wall in front of me, willing the light to go out. I'm afraid she'll see it so I grab her, flip her onto her knees, and pound into her from behind. She groans and cries out with each thrust. My hand glows brighter. I raise my hand and slap her ass, hoping to keep the light under control. With each smack, I thrust deeper and she just screams louder. I ball my glowing hand into a fist and slam into her one last time and fully release.

I roll off of her and onto my back. My hand reaches up to my shoulder wound. I can feel the tingle and sizzle as it closes over. My powers are back in full force. Why now? Why not with Mark? I need to get out of here before I turn Ginger's vagina into a flashlight.

I stand up, find my pants and throw them on. Ginger rolls over, her eyes wide, and points at my shoulder that's still smoking. "What the hell is that?"

I brush at the now healed wound. "Not sure I know what you're talking about."

"Your shoulder was literally smoking. The sex was good and all but come on."

I throw my shirt on and search for my jacket. "It's nothing. I get overheated sometimes."

She reaches toward me. "I'm sorry. Don't run off just yet. The sitter has the kids until morning."

Even if she was offering more sex, it wouldn't keep me. She's seen too much and my mind is jumping from her, to Mark, to…Barry. "Next time. I have to go check on Barry."

"Barry? Is that what you call your other lover?"

"Barry's not really my type. He's too spiritual."

"Well, make sure you leave your payment on the kitchen table on your way out." She pouts.

This woman is too much. "You've already taken all my cash. Put it on my tab." With that, I grab my jacket and head out.

Chapter 10

A wet tongue licks my ear to awaken me from sleep. A warm breath floats over me, panting with urgency and sends chills down my spine. Ginger must want another round but all I want is to sleep. My head feels like it's been caught in a blender. I keep my eyes closed and remain still, hoping she'll get the point.

Ginger's tongue is back in action flicking and playing with my ear. I moan and reach out toward her. The tongue moves to my hand, licking and massaging, tickling between each finger. This girl is kinky so I indulge. My eyes slowly open but instead of red flowing locks on a rocking stripper body, I see black hair, lots and lots of black hair. Maybe I picked up a different chick on the way home? Four legs, pointed ears, and a tail that curls upward is the physique sprawled across my couch. It's some sort of male husky mix, with a small spot of white located in the center of his chest. The tail wags back and forth and I'm greeted with a bark.

This is not the first time a stray has followed me home, but they never stay. Dogs find me depressing. He's sporting no collar or any other form of identification. I blink away the fog filling my head. Strikingly sky-blue eyes stare directly back at me and a cold, wet nose bumps my hand. I try to push him off the bed and he paws my arms and licks my hand again. He seems friendly.

I sit up and rub the sleep from my eyes to take in the crime scene laid out before me. Most of my boxes have been shredded and scattered across the floor. There's a half-eaten pizza box with what I hope is pizza sauce smeared into the carpet. Broken glass is everywhere and there are flakes of dried blood smeared on my skin. Pieces of glass stick out of my left hand and cuts cover that arm, alternating in different directions. I pull at the shards of glass and my right hand glows, closing the wounds. The cuts vanish before my eyes. The dog sits patiently waiting, wagging its tail. I point at the mess of cardboard scattered about the room. "I see that you had quite the night destroying all my shit, huh boy?"

"That was all you. Except for the pizza box, which was delicious."

"I guess that makes sense." I pause. Did this dog just talk to me? "You can talk?"

"Of course, I can talk."

There's an easy explanation for all of this. I am still drunk, high, or both. Hell, I'm probably still asleep and this is all a dream.

"This is not a dream and you're sober." He walks up and sniffs me. "Well, now you are. I'll explain later. Just open the door so I can piss or so help me I'll pick another spot in the corner."

Great. Now my place smells like dog and human piss. I stumble to the door. The dog dances around my feet, hopping up and down. I open the door and he bursts out to the nearest tree. He skids to a halt and lifts his leg. For almost a minute, he stands there and lets out a stream of piss that sprays the tree and drips down to the grass. He shakes off, runs back to me. I regretfully let him back inside.

I sit on the couch to collect myself. The dog sits in front of me and watches like he's waiting for something. Where do I even begin? I must be losing it. I should have drunk less, or maybe a whole lot more. Either way, I wouldn't be talking to a mutt. I run my hands through my hair. I can't drink less, so I grab a beer. "What's your deal? Do you belong to someone?"

"I'm my own dog."

Well at least I didn't steal him from someone. "Then where did you come from and why are you here? Help me out. I don't remember shit. I don't even know what day it is."

"Well, I can't help you there. They tell me I don't have a sense of time. Hold on a second." He reaches his back leg up and scratches behind his ear. "Much better. I was sent here to help you. It's ironic too because I'm here to tell you that you're running out of time."

I check my phone and the day says 'Wednesday'. That means I've been blacked out for at least 2 days with no recollection of what the hell happened to me. "Sent by who? Barry? Did Barry send you?" Oh, shit. Barry! I forgot about him.

"Barry's fine, and no he didn't send me. We went to visit him while you were under the influence. You kept doing something weird with your hands to him. Us more civilized species prefer the sniff the backend approach to say 'hello'. I thought he was your lover but when you were sleeping you were muttering something about Ginger. I work for the Big Man."

"Wait, you can hear my thoughts, too?"

"Yep. Even the dirty ones. Now, can you clean some of this mess so I don't step on any more glass? That stuff is impossible to get out of your paws when you don't have any thumbs."

I grab a dustpan from the closet and sweep up the glass, picking up the larger pieces with my bare hands. "Are you a Spot, Fido, or what?"

"Malakai. Call me Spot and you'll see just how obnoxious I can be."

I carry a full dustpan to the trash can and return to pick up more glass. It looks like I must have thrown a few bottles at the wall since there are dark liquid stains smeared down the wall. "Malakai? That's an unusual name for a dog."

"It means messenger of God. Seems fitting since that's who sent me."

I can't even begin to process what all this means. My head is in a fog with so many questions.

The dog cocks his head and speaks again. "I know this is a lot. The Boss thought it would be easier for you to relate to me. You always liked dogs in your past life so He thought a dog would help."

A loud, high-pitched repeated beep fills the air. The dog paces the room, runs to the door, and howls. "Make it stop. The beeping. It's so loud. Danger."

I walk over and see that the refrigerator door is still open. I close it and the beeping stops. "Better?"

He's huddled by the door shaking. "Sorry. I'm not used to all this dog stuff. High pitched noises trigger anxiety attacks. I also have these weird urges to howl along with any ambulance sirens."

I laugh at my strange new companion. "You said, 'past life'. So, I'm dead?"

"Not exactly."

"Then I'm alive?"

"Not exactly that either. You are what we would call…stuck. In limbo. I think you humans refer to it as purgatory."

I should have guessed this. The day after I shot myself, I woke up in my old college apartment back in the bad part of town with a hand that glowed. The suicide attempt felt real, but when I woke up the next day, I figured it was all just a bad dream. Purgatory means it's all real. I sit down on the floor and put my head between my legs. "It's all fuzzy. I remember being a doctor. I even remember the end. The rest though, is just pieces. Why purgatory? Why not send me to Hell where I belong?"

"That, I can answer. The Big Man wanted to give you a second chance. You had such talent in your past life as a doctor that He made you a Healer. Consider yourself lucky you didn't work a mundane factory or desk job."

"But everything feels so real. Especially the sex."

"As it should. This is all real. This is the world as you know. There are consequences to your actions. All the people you meet are real people. Only difference is they move on and you don't. Well, you and the other Healers."

"There's more like me? With my same powers?"

Malakai barks for what I take is agreement. "But you are wasting your talent. He gave you seven years and you used that time to drink, wander around aimlessly through town, heal a measly three people, and to play hours of Yahtzee with old ladies."

"I tried to heal Mark and it didn't work. Plus, those ladies love our afternoons together."

"You are being paid to heal every night, not just the nights you feel like it. He sent me to let you know that if you don't log enough heals in the next forty days, you will be stuck in purgatory forever."

I hate the idea of being stuck. The pressure of waiting to find out if I lost my license was too much. An eternity of doing the same thing every day would wear on me. Then again, at least I have sex and all the booze to keep me occupied.

The dog paws at my leg. "You may think it's fun now, but just think of how easily you get bored. Picture eternity with no purpose and nothing to move you forward. I suggest you listen to me and get your act together. Take me for a walk so I can show you a few things. Plus, I'm starving."

The fresh air will help to clear my head. "Uh, what do you eat?"

"I'm a dog. Dog food, you idiot. But I like pizza crust and hot dogs too."

"For a 'Messenger from God', you certainly have an attitude problem."

"I told you, I'm my own dog. Plus, the one with many names thought you would only listen to me if I matched your personality. You made me this way." He lifts his head in the air and sniffs. "Now, let's get going. I smell hot dogs." Long ropey strands of drool form at the corner of his lips and drip onto the carpet.

Gross. I'm about to head out the door when I pause. Malakai looks up at me. "What's the holdup?"

"People are going to think I'm crazy if they see me talking to a dog."

"People talk to their dogs all the time. But just in case, the Boss left a present with your envelope on the table."

On the cardboard box kitchen table is my daily allotted cash of a $100 and a small earpiece. I pick it up and see that it is a Bluetooth device. After a minute, I fit it in my ear. "I get it. Now, people will think I'm just talking on the phone."

"Good for you, and it only took you twice as long as a dog to figure that out. Now, can we go eat hot dogs already? I have a few things to show you before your next shift starts."

Chapter 11

There is nothing like the thick juicy taste of a street vendor hot dog, loaded New York style, with yellow mustard, kraut, and sautéed onions. It's the most satisfying bite with the slightest crunch from the outer casing and the explosion of meat juices that mix with the sourness of fermented cabbage. My taste buds sing with pleasure. If I'd known hot dogs would be present in the afterlife, I may have ended it sooner. The mutt sits next to me on the sidewalk, scarfing down two plain footlongs of his own.

I finish my food and wipe the mustard from the corners of my mouth. "Okay. So, you said God or whatever is giving me a second chance. At what? Life?"

"No, no. Once you're dead, that's it." Malakai hacks but then swallows whatever he was trying to bring up. "From what I understand, you had done enough good things in your life to warrant a trip to heaven. However, near the end of your life and really how you ended your life complicated things. So, we're going to see if we can get you back on track."

"This whole afterlife and heaven/hell deal, it's real?"

"Why do you seem so shocked? There are so many books and movies about it."

"Practicing as a doctor and being around death always made me question religion. I'm programed to put my faith in science and medicine. A life devoted to helping others seemed to be the most rewarding profession at the time. One mistake cost me everything."

"How's the afterlife been treating you?" Malakai turns his head and nibbles at his leg, satisfying an itch.

"I wound up in this shithole, looking like an old retired superhero or some washed up magician with a cheap light trick. It was all fun and games for the first few weeks. Then I got bored and decided I really didn't give a fuck anymore."

"Cue entrance of faithful canine spirit guide." Malakai belches and then stands up. "Purgatory offers you a second chance. Do enough good, you can flip the tides and end up running in fields filled with tennis balls, all the snack carts you can imagine and 500 virgins waiting around to rub your belly. If not, then it's lots of fire with rivers of snot, mountains made of nail clippings, and whatever else frightens humans. Oh, and cats. Hell is filled with cats."

Malakai trots down the street and I follow. He soon veers off, cutting down several alleyways until we end up somewhere familiar. My feet haven't walked these streets since I've been deceased. The storefronts haven't changed in seven years and my old hangout joint Canyon Pizza is still alive and kicking. I spent a large portion of my time pounding slices and beers within those walls. Thursday nights were quarter nights. The waiter would flip a coin and if you called it, the pie was free. Weekends the place was open until 4 am, serving up slices for a buck. The best cure for a hangover or a rough surgery. There was one time I remember Mark was so wasted he picked up a half-eaten slice off the sidewalk and ate it right up. He said he didn't want to wait in line.

Just a few buildings up is my old workplace, Blister City Medical. This is where Malakai halts. "Ummm, why are we here?"

"I wanted to start at the beginning. You're stuck in purgatory. Your one job is to go around healing people. The more heals, the more likely you are to stamp your passport out of here. Naturally, the best place to do that would be a hospital, right?"

"Right."

"It's not that simple. You are banned from entering all medical facilities. The Almighty is not a fan of the easy way out. If you had access to a hospital, you could log all your heals in one weekend. What lesson would you learn from that?"

"That sick and injured people go to the hospital."

Malakai reaches a paw up to scratch at the door. "Not all of them. Have you seen what healthcare costs nowadays? I don't count so well but I'm told it's a big pile of money. The Big Man doesn't like to interfere with earthly matters, but something had to be done. So, he created the 'Healers Initiative'."

"Me?"

"Yep. And all the poor souls like you who are meant to walk the streets helping those in need."

"Then why don't my powers work all the time?"

"We're getting there. Calm down, you're like a bitch in heat. Let's keep moving."

We turn back and head the way we came. The sun dips down in the sky, casting a red hue across the city. We make a left and head toward Barry's place. "So how many heals do I need?"

"Enough."

That's really helpful. I stop and pull down my jacket to show him one of my feather shaped scars. "Every time I heal someone, one of these suckers appears. So, if my skin is covered in them, do you think that's enough?"

He sniffs the scar and lick it a few times. "Those are meant to keep a tally on things. They add up until you get your wings."

"You can't be serious? Isn't that a little cliché?"

"I don't make the rules."

I pull my jack back up to cover the scars and we continue on down to Barry's. When we arrive, he is standing in his usual spot, this time holding a tambourine. He's smacking and shaking away, creating a unique sound I didn't think was possible with just a hand instrument. I approach him and slap him 'five'. "Play a song for me, Mr. Tambourine man."

He continues tapping and dancing away, alternating hands, and striking his hip. "Ah, you joke but this drum with jingles appeared before me while I slept. There are thoughts that it signifies a great surprise. I play it now in thanks from the streets."

Malakai wags his tail and looks at me. "This guy is hysterical. Are you going to frisk him now?"

"In a minute. You can't just approach a guy and feel him up without buying him dinner first."

Barry stops playing with his brow wrinkled and eyes squinting. He digs at the inside of his ears like he's searching for gold. "Scott, the medicine you provide is prescription grade stuff. I finished my last joint hours ago and I'm still feeling the effects. That dog of yours is talking again."

"Ah, I forgot that part," said Malakai. "Whenever Barry is high, he can understand me as well as other animals. You always thought he was crazy, and he still is. But there is some truth to his ramblings."

Barry sits down and reaches his hand out for Malakai to sniff. "It's okay, boy. Remember me from the other night?" Malakai trots up and licks his hand as Barry pets and scratches behind Malakai's ears. "So, what are you two up to tonight? Another night of wasted opportunities?"

"Actually, I'm working tonight."

"There is our great surprise. Scott is learning to care."

"I wouldn't go that far just yet." I motion for Barry to come closer. He huffs as he gets up and stretches out his arms for me to check him for hidden cash. I pat him down. "The canine is showing me the ways of my profession."

Malakai sniffs at Barry's right shoe. I point and Barry hands it over. Rolled up, jammed in the toe of the shoe is a twenty. I hold it up. "Damn, Barry. The tips must be getting better or you're becoming a stealthier pickpocket."

"You gave me that twenty just two nights ago when we negotiated a raise."

I looked to Malakai for guidance.

"Don't look at me," Malakai said. "I told you I can't count."

I finish with Barry and we make our typical trade-off of cash and a joint, this time back down to ten dollars and a single joint. "I know you have your eyes and ears out there, Barry. Where should Malakai and I sniff out trouble this evening?"

"No intel has been provided for tonight, but Saturday night that new mayor is making a public appearance. There's a charity event going down near the Spectrum Center. It would be wise if someone with your abilities were to make an appearance."

"Why? I thought everyone loved Mr. Popular? The papers say nothing but good things about his agenda."

"Don't question my instincts. I tell you only what I know. Security should be high but the cops are overworked. The city takes what it wants."

I whistle for Malakai who wandered off to chase pigeons. We leave Barry and continue on. Overhead street lamps blaze, lighting up the now dark sky. Large mutant brown and green beetles weave and scurry between my feet, racing for the safety of home. Even they know not to stay out too late. Most businesses close at sundown. It's not worth the risk of their business when the thugs come out to play.

Malakai sniffs and we head down Graham Street. We pass a small Chinese restaurant across from the railroad tracks that serves only takeout orders. The building is no larger than a standard kitchen. The open sign is always lit up and the parking lot is always empty. Malakai lifts his leg to piss on the side of the building.

"Must you do that?"

"Just marking the route." He finishes and grabs a piece of day-old dried up Szechuan chicken laying on the ground, a scrap that fell out from someone's take-out order. He swallows it down then trots back over toward me. "How did you know with Barry?"

"What do you mean?"

"How did you know you should heal him?"

"Gut instincts."

I knew Barry from my previous life. Back when I worked at Blister City Medical, he was always coming in there asking for prescription painkillers. He claimed he had a chronic condition, an old shoulder injury from when he was hit by a car as a kid. The other clinicians refused to see him, claimed he was just a junky looking for an easy score. Being a fresh out of medical school naïve doctor, I gave him the benefit of the doubt. I offered him a full work up if he wanted to continue to receive scripts. His insurance wouldn't cover it so I took some quick radiographs and didn't charge him. The x-rays showed an old fracture with tons of remodeling and OCD lesions, obvious evidence for chronic pain. Back when I was treating him, he didn't have track marks. This was before he chased the dragon.

"What happened to Barry?"

"Get out of my head. This is my story. I found him with a syringe sticking out of his arm, passed out in some back alleyway lying in his own piss. It was just a few days after I woke up, before I even knew about my little light trick. When I saw Barry lying there, I thought he was already dead. Barely recognized the bastard. I intended to keep on walking but instead, something stopped me. He looked familiar enough that I hovered over him to get a better look. My hand lit up and the rest was easy. Since I was the only one who would approve his prescription, he was forced to find other means of pain control with me being suddenly out of the picture."

A fly buzzes near my face and I swat it away. It dips down toward Malakai. He reaches out and snaps at the air with his teeth, catching the fly and swallowing it down. He wags his tail. I shake my head and we continue. "Is there a limit to the number of heals in a certain timeframe?"

"What do you mean?"

"Is there a recharge? A few days back, I ran into my friend from med school. He got himself caught up with the wrong guys and ended up getting his ass shot. When I went to heal him, the light didn't work."

"All I know is that you are only supposed to heal good people. And being that you're a night shift employee, you only get paid for heals after sunset."

We follow Graham Street down past the laundromat that leaves its door wide open at all times. The pavement has deep fissure lines that snake across the surface, breaking up the asphalt and causing potholes that fill with stagnant water. My feet trudge into these potholes, not bothering to step over them. I welcome the grim and the splash of gray water filled with soot. We pass an older lumber yard with palates of wood stacked high and scattered throughout the yard. A barbed wire fence surrounds the area, double layered at the top for insurance to snag anyone dumb enough to climb the fence.

"Get out of the fucking vehicle. Hands up. Now, before I blow your brains out."

The dog has led me right to trouble. Malakai and I hear the commotion and take off running in the direction of the voice. We travel south a few yards and hang a left onto Atando Street. Up ahead, a silver Honda Civic faces away from us. Malakai runs and jumps up. He slams his paws against the driver's side window and bears his teeth. Foamy drool smacks the window with each bark. An old man lies next to the car on the side of the road. The car tires squeal. Gravel and exhaust spray into my face as the car peels out, turns down the next street, and races away.

I look down at the older gentleman. He's dressed in khakis and a button-down shirt. What little hair sits on his head is white and wispy. A hematoma is forming on top of his head, clearly visible as a bruise through his thinning hair. He's covered in sweat and gravel. A little blood forms at the corner of his mouth. He's breathing but unconscious. Looks like the car thief punched him in the face and then cracked him over the head with the butt of a gun. I need to address the hematoma before the swelling causes any more damage.

Malakai sniffs the old man. "Should be a pretty easy one for you."

I kneel down and look around to check my surroundings. This area is filled with security lights and street lamps that keep everything well lit. I reach my right hand out over the top of the man's head but I pause.

"What are you waiting for?"

"I'm checking for shadows. The last time I tried this whole healing thing, it didn't end well. There was this darkness or form and it sort of swooped down and dove into the guy I was trying to heal. He never woke up."

"Umm, we're in a city at night. There are shadows everywhere."

"This one was different. It had a mind of its own."

"Don't be such a pussy. Now, hurry up and heal this guy before it's too late."

I open my hand and it immediately glows and heats up. The bruise fades and the blood dries by the man's mouth. He stirs and opens his eyes as my light still shines on him. I stop and reach down to help him up.

"What happened? Who are you? My car. Where's my car?"

"The name's Scott. Your car's been stolen. This is not the safest end of town and if I were you, I'd head straight home. Once you get there, call the police."

"You saved my life. What are you?"

"I'm still trying to figure that last part out." I wave him off, not answering any more questions. The man is still dazed so I pull out my burner phone for emergencies and call him a cab. We stand guard as he gets his bearings. He thanks me again as the cab pulls away.

The underside of my left forearm buzzes and I turn it over to see a small feather scar appear. The other scars are on `my back and shoulders, easily hidden from plain view. Great. This one's going to be harder to hide.

Malakai and I make our way back to Graham and continue further south, past a few abandoned warehouses. Each building is surrounded by the same two-layered barbwire fencing. We wander up and down the block for an hour or more. Up ahead, we come upon a rundown gas station up with an attached convenience store. Malakai halts. His hackles rise and his tail sticks straight up. He lets out a low growl. "Something doesn't smell right here. Let's check it out."

Having the mutt around is going to make filling my quota a piece of cake. Through the glass, we get a view of the chaos inside. Two men point guns and shout at a cashier with his hands in the air and back pressed up against the wall. Each man is wearing a brown paper bag over their face with small eye holes cut out. The cashier's hands shake and he tries to reach for something. The one masked gunman aims and fires. A security camera explodes from the wall, sending glass and other camera bits that rain down onto the counter. The cashier ducks down and pops up again with a shotgun. Bad move. The gunman fires again, this time hitting the cashier. His partner dives over the counter and grabs the cash from the register.

Blister City is out of control. There was a carjacking an hour ago a block over and now this? Are we trying to out Detroit, Detroit?

We head into the store just as the gunmen jet out the back, leaving us with the cashier lying on the floor in a blood-soaked shirt. He's holding his side. A gunshot wound to the abdomen is a slow kill. If by some miracle the bullet didn't strike a major artery, it was sure to rip open his guts, leaking intestinal juices and all the bacteria with it into his abdominal cavity. A septic abdomen is a terrible way to die.

The cashier is mumbling something and I lean closer. Something about him wanting me to call his wife and some sappy shit like that. He seems like a good soul. I look to Malakai.

"Your call," he says. "I'm going to grab snacks."

The overhead fluorescent lights flicker from a shorted fuse or faulty bulb. Then the temperature drops. A smoky whisp floats toward me inches off the ground. I shiver but focus on my task. My hand reaches out and glows. There's more heat and intensity than before. Even the cashier's abdomen lights up. His abdominal muscles push the bullet backward until it drops onto the floor, his skin closing behind it like the edges are being pulled together with suture when repairing a wound.

The shadow entity crawls toward us. It floats over the cashier's mouth. I wait for the hand to appear and for it to dive down the cashier's throat. But it doesn't. Not this time. Instead, it drifts closer, heading straight for me, a cloud drifting in midair. I try to move but I'm stuck in a trance, watching the shape as it rolls and shifts. The dark hand forms and reaches out toward me. I open my mouth to inhale.

All of a sudden, something grabs the back of my collar and pulls me back. The hand swipes and misses my face. Behind my back, I feel a thick fur coat.

"Run," Malakai screams.

Chapter 12

We race down another two city blocks and around a corner. There's an overhead stoop that I collapse underneath in an exhausted heap. My legs are rubber and it feels as if my lungs have been incinerated by the fire burning in my chest.

Malakai stands watch. His tongue hangs out in a soft pant. "What's wrong old man? Two legs not enough?"

What I hope is an insult response comes out as a garbled wheeze instead. My knees pull into my chest to ease my breaths. The middle of my spine stings as another feather scar appears. Finally, my respirations slow to where I can speak. "What was that? Why were we running?"

"Because you were about to be terminated. It looked like you had fallen off the Absinthe liquor wagon before I pulled you away. That shade almost had you."

"That creepy smoky shadow thing?"

"Yes, shades."

"One of them took Mark. It snaked its way into his mouth, causing him to expire. There was nothing I could do."

"Yeah, well you were about to breathe one in. Do that and you've bought yourself a one-way ticket to the underworld."

I stand and brush the dirt off, discarding a few wet cigarette butts smashed into my jeans. "I thought I couldn't die in purgatory?"

"Well, you're already dead. Shades are nasty evil beings. They can take a life and erase people in purgatory."

"How do I avoid them?"

"You can't. They're remnants of past souls who have moved on to the underworld. They're a whole ten sorts of evil. The faster you log your heals, the less you need to worry about them."

We limp home to get some rest. The next night we choose different streets to wander up and down. It's a slow night but we find a few more people. Some I heal, some I don't. There's one rich guy who gets the royal snot beat out of him during a routine robbery. It's an unfair fight but he's the kind of prick who wears a bowtie and bowler hat in the ghetto. Something inside me senses he's a waste to society as my hand doesn't even feel lukewarm around him. I almost feel bad for him as we leave him in his misery. Almost.

The sky switches to an orange glow with a new morning, sending the scum scurrying back into the shadows. The heat of the early morning sun dries all bodily fluids spilled from last night, leaving only flakes of sticky brick red stains on my jeans that will get mistaken for mud. My knuckles are split open once again, but the blood that remains caked in the cracks is not my own. Malakai gives his body a good shake, his black fur hiding evidence of where we've been. I tell him we've earned a sit-down breakfast after working two nights in a row so we head in the direction of Angelina's Café.

The sign over the café shorts a fuse so only part of the letters light up. Malakai cocks his head and reads the sign. "Angel Café, huh? This place looks a little too fancy for you, Scott."

"Don't you worry. This place is a dive but the food is fantastic."

The door squeaks open and we slip in. Smoke billows up out of the kitchen and I can hear choking and sputtering. The chef steps out from the kitchen, fanning his apron while still coughing. He looks at me and waves. I grab my usual paper and booth. Malakai trots after, jumping into the seat across from me.

A girl with blonde pigtails skips over to our table wearing a waitress apron that hangs below her knees. She hands us each a menu. Her cheeks are flushed and she wears a huge smile on her face that stretches from ear to ear. She can't be more than seven years old. I stand to scan the restaurant, wondering where the kid came from. There is only one other customer in the joint and it's one of the regulars.

Her striking blue eyes stare, moving back and forth between Malakai and I. Those eyes look oddly familiar. I wait a minute, thinking some parent will come to claim this kid but they don't. Finally, the silence gets to me and I look back at her. "May I help you?"

"Can I pet your dog?"

"I don't know, ask him." Malakai opens his mouth like he's about to say something. I point directly at him. "Don't you dare." He shuts his yapper.

Malakai bows down to lick her hands and face. She reaches her small hands up and buries them deep into his thick, dark coat.

Nancy approaches the table and sets a cup down in from of me of steaming hot coffee. "Layla, stop bothering the customers. I told you to stay behind the counter."

"But Mom, I asked first. I'm just petting the dog."

Nancy points her finger. "Counter, now. And take off my apron."

The young girl pouts but follows her mother's orders handing over the too large apron and retreating back behind the counter.

I look up at Nancy and raise a questioning eyebrow. "Mom, huh?"

"The sitter was sick and I had no one to watch her. She's usually better about leaving customers alone. When did you get a dog?"

"He's my service animal."

"No worries. Have you seen the inside of this place? I'm sure he's cleaner than most of the customers that walk through here." She reaches in her apron and flips out her little notepad. Her hand rests on my shoulder. "So, what'll it be, Scottie?"

"The special. Make that two. My furry friend has earned himself a well-cooked meal."

"Ha. You really want the special today? Did you see the amount of smoke coming out of the kitchen earlier?"

"Good point. Fine, we'll make it easy on the chef. Two Dots and a Dash and a Shingle with a shimmy and a shake. Make it a double order. I guess a bowl of dog soup for my friend as well."

"Only the best for you." She winks and sashays off back to the kitchen. I turn to watch her walk away, my eyes set on that perfect tight ass. Malakai puts his paw up on the table. "Not that I mind, but what the hell did you just order me? Dog soup?"

"Relax. It's just water." Nancy turns to catch me staring and I give her one of my token looks. She's still not my type, but I'd be lying if I said I didn't want to tap that at least twice.

"Can you make it any more obvious?" Malakai startles me and I turn back toward our table.

"Huh?"

"The waitress. You want to bang her."

"Whatever. She's not my type."

"Uh, huh. Could have fooled me. Is Ginger your pet name for her?"

"What?"

"When I first found you, all passed out and doped up on who knows what, you kept muttering Mark and Ginger in your sleep."

"Ginger's my weekend girl. You'll meet her soon enough."

"Ha. You don't have cojones to handle even one girl."

"Watch it, or you're sleeping outside tonight." My hand rests on the newspaper. I flip it over to check the headlines. The front page is dedicated to the upcoming charity gala this weekend. It states that many of Blister City's public figures will be in attendance, including Mayor Jeff Poplar. His mug is plastered right under the headline. I point to the picture and hold it out to show Malakai. "This is that gala Barry was yammering on about that we're supposed to check out tomorrow night."

Malakai smells the paper. "Smells suspicious."

"It's a newspaper. I met the mayor once. His taste in strippers is questionable, but at least he's trying to help the city. I'm sure the place will be swimming with security but Barry's voices feed him good predictions. We'll swing by Saturday night to sniff things out."

"You leave all the sniffing to me."

I feel a small tap on the back of my shoulder and turn to see the same blue-eyed blonde pigtailed girl from earlier. She has her hands clasped behind her and is rocking back and forth on her feet.

"Mister? Can I sit with you and your dog?"

"Aren't you going to get in trouble with your mom?"

"Not if you don't tell her."

I slide over and she parks herself right next to me. She points at my knuckles, all split open and bruised.

"Did that hurt?"

"Not as much as you would think."

Nancy returns and the girl slips under the table out of sight. She sets down two plates of fried eggs, bacon and toast with jam in front of both me and Malakai. Malakai doesn't wait for the plate to touch the table before he scarfs the food down. Nancy peeks under the table to see her daughter. "Nice Try. Back to where you belong."

I intercept her. "It's alright, Nancy. I told her to sit with me."

Nancy gives me a look like she knows I'm covering for the girl but buys in. "Alright. But if she is too much, just holler for me."

I take a bite of my food and nod. Malakai has licked every last speck of crumb from his plate. He eyes my food. A long string of drool drips down and hits the table. I tell him he's gross and to get ahold of himself. If he touches my food, I'll send him to doggie heaven.

"Hey, Mister?" The girl occupies herself by folding a napkin from the dispenser in little squares. "Do you like my mom?"

"Of course. She is a very nice person."

"Are you going to date her?"

"I'm not sure your mom likes me that way."

"She said you come in here just about every morning and only sit in her section. She talks about you a lot."

"What about your father?"

She stops folding her paper and stares down at her hands. "I don't have one. Mom says he died when I was just a baby."

"I'm sorry to hear that."

"It's okay. I don't remember him. Mom still gets sad about it sometimes."

"How'd he die?" I take a big bite of chewy bacon and grab my coffee to wash it down.

She keeps her head lowered. "I'm not supposed to know this but Mom and Grammy still talk about it a lot. He died at a hospital. Grammy says it was one of them drinking doctors that did it."

My coffee flows down the wrong pipe, sending me into a coughing spasm. I look directly into the little girls piercing blue eyes, the same eyes that still haunt me seven years later. "Layla, what's your last name?" My mind begs her not to say 'Caldwell'. My luck can't be that terrible.

"Caldwell."

I look across and see Nancy watching us. My throat tightens. The walls close in and the room spins and tips. Beads of sweat form on my brow. Malakai senses my urgency to get the hell out of there and he jumps down from his seat. I pull out a handful of bills, everything in my pocket, and throw it down on the table. Salty bacon and eggs rise up the back of my throat. I mutter something about feeling ill and Layla lets me out.

I stumble out the door just in time before losing my breakfast all over the side of the building; yellow yolk mixed with green stomach juices.

"Dude, what the hell was that? You have to warn me when you're going to have a freakout moment like that," says Malakai.

"The girl. Nancy. I killed him."

"What are you talking about? You killed who?"

"I'm the drunk doctor that killed Kevin Caldwell."

"Oh…that seems important". He eyes the vomit, "So, are you going to eat that?"

Chapter 13

"Paging Dr. Scott Weaver. Dr. Weaver report to surgery, please. Dr. Weaver to surgery."

The yellow crusted paste of sleep collects in the corners of my eyes. I yawn and wipe it away. There's a dry gritty taste in my mouth like my tongue is covered in sandpaper. A large cup of black coffee warms my cold hands, the heat seeping through the thin cardboard cup. My vision is fuzzy and it takes a few more sips to clear my head. My evening attire consists of green wrinkled scrubs decorated in old blood splatter with a small lab coat thrown over top buttoned sideways with sleeves ending mid forearm. The hair on my head is flattened on one side. It's the complete just rolled out of bed look.

The surgery prep area is bustling with activity. Nurses hustle about, priming IV lines and opening surgical packs. The brightness of the overhead fluorescent lights burns my retinas. I squint. One of the surgical nurses looks me up and down.

"Are you okay?"

"Fine!" I snap. The nurse jumps, the answer coming off a little harsh. Another sip of coffee to collect myself. I lower my tone. "Where is Mark?"

"Who? Dr. Andrews?"

I nod. "The one you were supposed to call. He's working tonight, not me." My words slur. I take another drink of coffee.

"We couldn't get ahold of him and Dr. Kidwell's out of town on CE. You were next on the list. We've had several emergencies and we're short-handed. Are you sure you're okay? Do you need to eat something or an IV bag for yourself?"

She must smell the wine still on my breath. "I'm fucking here, aren't I?" I stop myself. It's 2 am and this poor girl is only doing her job. "Sorry, I'm just tired from being on-call the past three nights. Catch me up so we can get started."

She nods and grabs the closest clipboard and rambles off cases as quickly as possible. My mind won't focus. I stare at the floor, the wall, my coffee, her shoes, my shoes…

"Dr. Weaver, are you listening?"

"Yep. Patients sick and dying. Blah, blah."

"I asked you which one you wanted to start with? Are you sure you're okay? Do you want me to call someone else in here?"

"Is there anyone else?"

She shakes her head.

I look her dead in the eyes. "Then stop asking me that. Basic triage 101. Whichever case you feel is most critical, then we'll start with that one."

"Dr. Stevens is currently in surgery with a gunshot to the chest. There's another gunshot to the abdomen and his vitals aren't great. I'm thinking early sepsis from a leaking bowel. There's also a young girl with a bullet wound to the face. She seems to be in a lot of pain but her vitals are fairly stable. But there are three other gunshot victims still in processing and we just got a call that they are airlifting two more in as we speak."

"What the hell happened?" We are going to be here all night.

"According to one of the receptionists up front, two gentlemen got into a dispute outside a recording studio in the Music Factory. They were both armed and most of their shots were directed toward the outdoor beer garden next door. Both gunmen are dead. It could

have been so much worse. That beer garden is always packed and tonight they were hosting a kid's birthday party."

"Wait, a kid's birthday party at a beer garden?"

"You know Blister City. Can't go to a brewery or bar without running into children. So, which case first, Dr. Weaver?"

The septic abdomen is going to take me half the night. My head's still a little fuzzy so I down the rest of the coffee in one swig. I need something quick to wake me up. "Prep the gunshot to the face."

"Are you sure Dr. Weaver? She is stable and it's just a little shrapnel, wasn't even a direct hit."

"Then it shouldn't take me very long. Get me the girl first. In the meantime, start the abdominal wound on fluids and hit him with a dose of Unasyn and Metronidazole."

I finish the last stitch on the girl and check the clock. Seventy-five minutes have passed. Damn, that took forever and she'll still need several follow-ups with a plastic surgeon. A wound like that normally takes me thirty minutes max. The nurses take her to recovery. They roll in the gunshot to the abdomen and I rescrub. My head is spinning and I'm nauseated. Just need to focus and power through.

I open him up and the nurse's suspicions were correct. His bowels are leaking and peritonitis is already setting in. I instruct them to pour liter after liter of warm fluids into his abdomen to flush out what we can. "I need more damn suction over here, now. I can't see anything."

My assistant repositions the tube and clears my view. The healthy sections are repaired. The worse section of bowel is muddy in color, leaving me to perform a resection and anastomosis in order to reattach two healthy remaining areas of bowel together. The seal holds, but now there's a steady bloody ooze. I don't know where it's coming from.

"Dr. Weaver, his pressures are tanking."

"Increase his fluid rate." I keep searching. I push the intestines out of the way and watch the spleen for signs of hemorrhage.

"We're cutting his gas down!"

"Not yet." I keep digging.

"Dr. Weaver…"

"Just a minute. I almost have it. I think I see the bullet." There it is, right next to the superior mesenteric artery. I ask for hemostats and reach in slowly.

"Dr. Weaver leave the bullet. It's too risky."

"I can handle it, damn it."

"You've been staring at the bullet for five minutes. Close him up, now. We'll wait until he's more stable."

"I said, I got it."

My hands are shaking. My vision is blurred and sweat drips down beneath my mask. I taste the salt of my own sweat and I gag, dry heaving into my mouth. I reach in again and grab the bullet. One slip in either direction and I could nick the artery. I pull with slow, steady traction and the bullet releases. "Got you, you asshole."

Right where the bullet was the oozing changes to a fast and pulsing flow. Fuck. I must have slipped and severed the artery. I grab hemostats and clamp, grasping whatever I can. There's so much blood.

"He's slipping into V fib…grab the paddles. Dr. Weaver, step back."

"No, I got this. Hand me the hemoclips and the gelfoam."

"That's not going to do it. Back away now or I will shock you. We're losing him."

"One more second…"

"We don't have a second. CLEAR!"

He lifts up off the table with the shock. They keep working on him, adjusting the paddles to a higher and higher dose. It won't matter. He's already gone. This one's on me. It's all my fault. I have to be the one to tell this poor guy's wife, mother, father, brother, or whoever the hell else cares about this guy that I was the asshole who let him die.

"Dr. Weaver, we need you to call it."

"One more time, dammit."

"Dr. Weaver…"

"Patient number 57932, Mr. Kevin Caldwell, time of death is 4:32 am."

Chapter 14

Long shadows creep across the carpet to cover up my face, stirring me from sleep. I open my mouth, hoping they'll take me now. Unfortunately, these are normal, meant to show the passage of the sun and not the transition to the underworld.

Malakai watches me from across the room. "What the hell was that?"

"Huh?"

"I barely got you back to the apartment. You were vomiting all exorcist style and then you wouldn't stop howling. I never saw such a sad display from a sober client before. They warned me post-suicidals were depressing but I wasn't prepared for this. You're lucky us dogs are so loyal or I would have left you in a blubbering heap."

I rub the sleep from my eyes and sit up on the couch. "How long was I out?"

"I still can't tell time, dumbass. Based on how hungry I am, I'd say it's been weeks."

"Aren't you always hungry?"

"Fair point. We should really get back to work so you can get me more snacks."

"But I killed her father?"

"Who?"

"The girl at the diner. The waitress's daughter. I killed her father."

Layla's face pops into my head with her pigtails and that sassy little attitude. Those piercing blue eyes just like her father. I've ruined their lives. That poor little girl won't have the joyful embarrassment that comes from having a father make her boyfriend piss his pants in fear when he comes to take her to her first dance. Her mother has to work in a shitty diner for meager tips because of me. She will never know the relief of having a husband come home and say 'I'll take the kid out for a stroll so you can have a moment alone.' How can I show my disgraceful face to them again? Ugh, but where else will I find dinner and a show on the cheap?

"You need to end this pity party of one. You'll never move on if you can't let go of your old life."

Malakai has no idea what I'm going through. Or, he does, and that is why he was sent to guide me on my path. I look at him straight on and make an executive decision. "No work tonight. I'm getting plastered again."

"He isn't going to like this. Forty days was all you get. Do I need to remind you about being stuck here forever to live with your mistakes?"

"Honestly, who cares what He thinks. I need a drink and to get laid." I sniff my shirt. The stench of sweat and vomit mix together to create a cologne in the scent of 'who gives a fuck'. There's a new hole, right over my chest. It could be from wear, or from a bullet. It doesn't even matter at this point. I pull the shirt off, flip it inside out, and put it back on.

"You need to get back to healing."

I head to the kitchen to collect my allowance. In the drawer where I keep Barry's medicine is the pick-me-up I need, hidden away for just this sort of emergency. My hand is on a buried treasure hunt, sifting through an odd assortment of pens, rolled joints, beer bottle caps, and take-out menus. The container is small round plastic, like a lip balm container a little girl would keep in her purse. I twist the cap to reveal my sweet white powdered candy.

Malakai pulls on my pant legs. "Absolutely not. Release. Let it go."

"Look, we both know how this ends, me not giving a fuck. You can come with or stay here. Be a good boy and I may even give you a lick." A small sniff and an extra fingerful to brush across my gums and I'm good to go. I pocket the container. With a final lick, hope and despair are simultaneously ratcheted up to levels the mentally sane couldn't possibly understand."

"You can't bring that flea-ridden mutt in here. This is a place of business." The bouncer at Mustang Jenny's folds his arms and blocks the doorway.

"It's a strip club. Look at that guy in the corner. He's jerking it as we speak. Come on man, he's my service animal." I take a step to the side to walk around him.

He shifts and his hand pushes me back. "You're here all the time. I've never see you with a service animal."

The nerve of some people, questioning fake disabilities. "He's my emotional support animal. He had a harness, but he ate it."

He crosses his arms over his chest and looks me up and down. Eventually, he steps to the side to let us pass. "Whatever man. But if he bites anyone or pisses on anything, I'm going to bite and piss on you."

I turn toward the mutt. "Hear that Malakai, be a good boy."

Malakai looks up at me and lets out a low growl. I grab his muzzle and hug him next to me. "Aww, he says thanks."

I grab a drink. Communal bowls of popcorn, peanuts, and Cheetos are dispersed at the bar. I grab a handful of stale bar popcorn, with extra seasoning from piss soaked hands, and feed it to Malakai. A few pieces make it into my mouth as well. My teeth stick to the Styrofoam-like texture of the kernels, flattening what should normally crunch. I ask the barkeep if Ginger's working tonight and he points her out.

She's serving drinks to a few tables in the far corner. Ass-hugging shorts and a tube top that leaves her midsection bare are her evening attire. It's a little early yet for her high-diving acrobatic routine. My funds are limited since I gave most of my cash to the waitress back at the diner. Not enough for a lap dance. Instead, I stalk her from a distance. She's smiling, flirting with the other men. Her hand caresses their shoulders and she leans over when they speak, tits hovering in their faces. She's works them hard to make me jealous, and then looks up as if she's surprised to see me.

Malakai paws at my leg. He's watching me eye the stripper. My leg bounces and I fiddle with my glass. I nod toward her. "That's her. She's my girl."

"Whatever is running through your veins right now must be giving you a false sense of confidence because there is no way you could get a girl like that."

I'm lacking the sense of an inhibition with enough energy to run through a wall, or at least show off to a dog. "I'll prove it. Stay."

She's still bent over with her tits bouncing all free and braless in some schmuck's face. It's working. He reaches for his wallet but I grab her arm, leading her away from the table and toward the exit.

"Hey, get your hands off her." The bouncer that gave me trouble at the door sees us. I've seen that look in his eyes before. This might not be the best time for courageous acts of stupidity.

He moves fast, barreling right toward us. This isn't our first fist pounding encounter. My eyes close and wait for the beating, but it doesn't come.

Instead, Ginger stops him. "It's okay, Jerry. I know him. Give me a few minutes."

He furrows his brow and grunts. It's a warning. He listens to Ginger and backs off as I drag her the rest of the way out of the door.

She throws my hands off her. "What is your problem? I'm working. You can't play jealous boyfriend in front of customers or I'm going to get fired."

I push her into the wall with her hands pinned above her head. My hips thrust into hers, making sure she can feel what I want. With one finger, I trace the outline of her lips and stop to hush her. "Keep quiet. This won't take long."

Her hands push me back. "Not now. Someone will see us."

"There's no one out here. Just real quick." I lean in and kiss her neck. "I missed you." My jacket falls to the ground, landing in the gravel.

"Oh, and that makes up for you leaving and then never calling me?"

My mouth finds her earlobe and I suck, flicking it with my tongue. She stays still. I stick my hand beneath her shorts and feel, testing her out. She adjusts her stance to let my fingers slip in where she's already wet. I pull at her shorts, ripping them down to her knees. She takes the bait, works at my jeans, undoes the button and pulls the zipper.

I thrust into her and she inhales as she's pushed up against the brick wall. She doesn't stop me but takes every inch of me in submission. Overhead security lights illuminate the trash bin next to us but we stay hidden in shame. It's different than the other night, more urgent, forced. I grunt but she's silent. A few more pumps and I finish.

Her face is a look of concern rather than pleasure. She asks if I have a napkin or something so she can clean herself. I take off my shirt and hand it to her. She wrinkles her nose but grabs it and wipes between her legs. As she does, she stares at my scars. There's more than the last time she saw them.

She pulls up her shorts and hands the shirt back to me but I don't put it on. "Well that was…cheap, degrading, and short. Are you okay?"

"I'm fine." I'm not fine.

"Okay. You seem distracted I guess, jittery."

I pick my jacket up and pretend that I care about wiping the dust off. "Look, we don't have to do this thing. I can find another whore to get me off."

Her knee jerks up and nails me right in the crotch. "You're just like every other asshole that comes in this joint."

I'm doubled over gasping for breaths, enjoying the pain, enjoying the ability to feel anything. I manage to cough out, "Walk you home?"

"Are you kidding me? What do you think?"

I shrug. She's right but tonight is light on caring. I keep my shirt and jacket tucked under my arm and walk away.

"Wait! Where are you going? We need to settle this."

Avoidance is the best answer with women. I wave goodbye over my shoulder without bothering to turn around. The door slams shut. She's gone back inside. I head to the front entrance and whistle for Malakai. He runs out of the door, trotting up to walk beside me.

"What kind of creeper are you? That poor girl ran back in there crying her eyes out."

"I don't want to talk about it." He's right. Never should have gotten tangled up with the woman. If she never speaks to me again, I'll understand.

"So, do you want to just call it a night?"

"Not yet. I'm still sober enough to remember. We're going to The Underground."

Malakai trails me as we take a few streets over to Sugar Creek. The street lights overhead are dark from broken bulbs that were never replaced. We're guided by only the moon and my internal compass to stir up trouble. We finally walk up to the familiar shack of a bar. If not for the cars out front, I'd think it was abandoned. Even the sign overhead isn't turned on.

We enter and find a place at the bar. I'm still not wearing a shirt but no one notices a half-naked man with a dog in this place. The barkeep asks for our order and I point at anonymous brown liquid number five. He grabs a glass, spits in it, wipes it out with a rag that's gray but was white at one point. The pour is generous and he slides the glass in my direction. I drain it in one long gulp. It refills right in front of my eyes. This bar tender is either a magician or I'm starting to feel the effects of this fine drink.

I ask him if he's seen my friends from the other night, the two large thugs that killed Mark. He nods to the end of the bar. There's a man hunched over, cap pulled down low so his face is covered. His sleeves are rolled up enough that I can make out the skull pirate tattoo. This is why I'm here.

Malakai senses my energy and he looks over at the thug. "You know I can read your thoughts. Bad boy. Murder is still one of the deadly sins that will punch your ticket to hell. Scott, no good can come from this."

"You're right."

I down the second glass of liquor and head over, target set on skull tattoo. The way he's hunched, he wants to be left alone. I prescribe some friendly company. My feet stumble at the last second and I shove into him just as he's lifting his glass to take a drink. It spills, splashing him in the face.

"Hey! Watch it, asshole."

I play it off like a sloppy drunk although my internal meter now reads stone sober. A firm slap on his back and he cringes. "Sorry about that man. Must have tripped."

He grunts and turns away but doesn't get away that easily. I drape my arm around his shoulders and motion for the barman. "Can I get another for my friend here? On me." My hand grabs his arm, right near the skull tattoo. "Whoa, what a cool tattoo. I bet all the ladies are like 'I want a piece of that pirate booty."

I have his attention now. He stands and shoves me off my barstool. "What's your problem?"

I catch myself before hitting the floor and push back. "You are. You think you can just go around killing whoever. No one is dumb enough to stop you because you're a big fucking oaf. Until now."

"What are you talking about?"

"Mark. The skinny blonde guy, you shot a few nights ago?"

"That loser? When you're a runner and can't pay your debts, shit gets real. He was given fair warning."

My fist smashes into his jaw. My carpal bones crumble from the impact as if I had just punched a steel I-beam. Previously scabbed knuckles split open, allowing blood to bubble up from underneath. The thug doesn't even waver.

Malakai grabs my pant leg and pulls back. He lets out a sharp bark.

My feet find purchase as I wait for the beating, craving the metallic taste of blood in my mouth. The thug's a little slow to react but when he lands the first shot, my lip explodes. I can feel my teeth shift during impact. The blood fills my mouth. I spit it right back on his shirt. Two more blows to my face and my vision is masked by my eyelid that begins to swell. Like a boxer on the verge of knockout in the final round, I sway but stay on my feet, begging for just one more hit.

I don't get what I want. The barkeep must not want to deal with the clean up so he drags me outside. He tells me to walk it off. I'm tempted to go back inside but he pushes me in the opposite direction. So, I walk.

I lurch forward, weaving back and forth. I'm going to pass out but my feet keep moving, heading further away from home down Sugar Creek. Malakai follows. In my pocket I discover the little round container filled with magic fairy dust. We pass by a gas station on the right. The lights are still on here. Bugs flutter and smack into the light, attracted to repeat the process over and over again. Under this display, I pause to unscrew the cap and sprinkle a line across the back of my hand. One good long snort and I feel my vessels constrict.

From the ground, a shade rises up toward me. It floats, suspended in midair, snaking back and forth. It calls me to the overpass across the way and I follow. My feet find the edge and with the interstate below. Even late at night, the road is busy with traffic zipping by underneath.

Malakai watches me from below. "What the hell do you think you're doing?"

I'm pushed up against the rail that sits waist high. My hands stretch out to the side. I let the wind whip over me. "I wonder what it would be like to fly."

"One bump of coke and you think you're a superhero? Nope. Not going to happen. Down."

There's a faint whisper in the wind, soft and soothing. It's coming from the shade.

Jump.

I need to know what it would feel like to be free, to float away from all my worries. The cars continue to zip by below. If the impact doesn't kill me a passing car is sure to do the trick.

The shade spins around my head, surrounding me in a smoky fog.

Jump.

I lean out further, tipping, allowing gravity to take me.

"Scott!"

I'm free, soaring like a bird off into the night. My arms flap and I rack my brain for 'happy thoughts', but forget that I have none. The ground rises faster and faster until my face meets it.

Chapter 15

It's peaceful here. The soft hum of a motor lulls me in and out of sleep. The corners of my mouth pull up into a foreign position. I'm smiling for once. It's nice. Then I hear something odd; a moist lip smacking/licking. I attempt to open my eyes, but only one opens. The other is matted shut. There's a large swelling over it and it's caked with a sticky goo that I take for blood. A black dog with white markings sits with his back toward me. Well, shit.

I tap the mutt with my foot. "Since you're here making that disgusting noise, I take it I wasn't successful in my leap of faith?"

Malakai turns his head toward me. "You can't die twice. That would be ridiculous. So, you might as well stop trying."

"The shade spoke to me. Its voice was an overpowering whisper, like I couldn't focus on anything else."

"Did it ever occur to you that listening to a talking shadow is a bad idea?"

I roll over on the couch and pull the blanket up to cover my face. Malakai grabs it and rips it away. He takes a corner in his mouth and grinds it with his teeth. The blanket shreds and he swallows a strip, slurping it down like spaghetti.

"Don't eat that. You'll just puke it up later."

"Then get up and take it away from me."

When he chews on it again, I finally sit up and rip it away. My hand inspects my eye and I feel the warm touch of the light as it absorbs the swelling, shrinking my eye back to normal. I blink several times and shake some sense back into my head.

"Hey, how did I get back here anyway?"

"Well, it wasn't easy. I managed to drag you to the side of the road after almost being hit by several cars. But that was the furthest I got. Your face was so smashed I would have taken you for a stranger and barked in any other situation. I retrieved Barry and he used your powers to fix your face. We left the black eye because it made you look tough. He carried you back home and helped himself to a few joints before he left."

I head to the kitchen for a quick inventory check. Barry cleaned me out. Not a single joint remains. I gather up my paycheck and find a new note with it. This one reads, "32 days left. Time to get back to work."

Malakai is sitting with his head hanging low. The corners of his mouth pull tight and a long string of drool falls to the carpet. His body lurches a few times and he barfs up the chewed blanket onto the carpet. He shakes himself off and stretches out across the carpet, belly crawling toward me.

"Worth it."

Malakai and I wait outside the Spectrum Center. As expected, security's been ramped up with police lining every corner. Some areas are roped off with yellow rolled security tape to keep the chaos to a minimum. We can hear applause from the crowd inside.

Two nearby officers keep a close eye on us. They're probably wondering what sort of trouble a blind man and his seeing eye dog could cause. Maybe wearing sunglasses at night wasn't a great call on my part. I'm sweating my balls off out here because I thought it was wise to keep my jacket on to hide my scars. I open it and hold it away from my body to show the cops I'm not hiding any bombs strapped to my chest. The officers look away.

Malakai yawns. "How long do we have to wait out here? I'm so bored."

I shrug. My legs bounce and fingers tap. I need a drink or a hit or a bump, something to keep me occupied.

Malakai watches me as I reach into my pockets, counting my loose change. "Oh no you don't. Bad."

"What?"

"You're staying sober tonight. This is a public figure we're guarding. I need you clear headed with no distractions."

"Fine." I replace the change and reach in my other pocket to pull out my phone.

"What are you doing now?"

I punch digits. "Calling Ginger to see if she's home. I'll steal some flowers and go apologize in person. Chicks love that shit. She's only a few blocks south of here." Malakai reaches out and bites my hand that's holding my phone. I drop it. "Ouch. Don't make me take you to animal control."

"What did I say? No distractions." Just then the doors of the Spectrum Center open and some of the patrons flood the streets. "Perfect timing."

Couples dressed to the nines walk hand in hand, groups of friends talk and laugh together, and for a moment I forget about all the shit going on in the world. Here is where all the rich of Blister City gather to donate their money to a charitable organization. This is where they come to feel good about themselves. Don't get me wrong, I'm in favor of these events. This used to be my Saturday night. But when you've been on the other side you see who else is here, lurking in the shadows. It's the people down on their luck, with that certain itch, forced to commit crimes. They wait to take advantage of a bunch of people with their guards down, under the influence of alcohol and high on feeling good about themselves. This is when the rich forget to look both ways. They forget which areas they are supposed to avoid at this time of night.

Exiting the building now is a man I recognize from the news. He's smiling and shaking hands with the group of suits surrounding him. His Hollywood-style smile glows against the backdrop of his fake spray tan and bleached blonde hair. His stylist must be stuck in the 90s. This is our man, Mayor Jeff Poplar.

"So, do we just follow him or what?"

Malakai isn't watching. Instead, he's found something stale or rotten to eat off the ground. He immediately hacks it back up. "Why are you asking me?"

"Aren't you here to help?"

"Since when do you listen to me? I guess you could follow him so you can be there if something does happen. Then you can heal him and we can get on with the evening. Don't try anything too heroic. Leave that up to the police."

The mayor breaks off from his posse. An all-black sedan with tinted windows pulls up toward him. No windows roll down. The mayor reaches for the handle of the back door. He steadies himself and grabs the handle more securely, opening the door and crawling in the back seat.

"There. He's in his car. We're good to go." I turn and walk away.

Malakai does not follow. He sniffs the air with his ears pinned back on his head. "Something doesn't smell right here. There's a third man in the car. I can smell him."

"It's probably just a bodyguard."

He's still sniffing. "No. He doesn't smell like the rest of the people inside. He smells off like soured meat. Let's go while the scent is fresh."

It's so hot the bottom of my shoes melt and stick to the pavement with each step as we jog after the car. It heads up Trade Street. Luckily, there are too many lights for them to gain any real distance on us. I wheeze and the sweat drips from my face. Malakai pants hard beside me as we stop for a breather.

The car takes a sudden left and I know where they're headed, good old Sugar Creek. No traffic signals to slow them down. No lights to show their sins.

I inhale and pick up the pace, now grateful I didn't down a six pack before because I would have puked seven times already. My sides heave in protest. I need to get in shape or find an easier method of transport.

POP. POP. POP.

Malakai and I glance at each other and run with everything we've got, fueled by adrenaline. Wheels screech and we watch the sedan hang a right and speed off up Graham Street. We'll never catch them now.

I stop and bend over with my hands on my knees, willing my lungs to suck in enough air to keep me from passing out. Malakai runs back and forth, his nose pinned to the ground. He pauses, lifts his front leg, and turns toward a ditch off the side of the road. There's something lying in that ditch. He barks, signaling me forward.

There curled in the ditch is our friend, the mayor. He's not moving. We're either too late or he's unconscious. I reach down and check for a pulse. Unconscious.

I give him the once over, assess the situation. Blood drips down the side of his face and seems to be coming from a head wound. At least two of the bullets struck home, one in the chest and one in the abdomen. This will take some effort but I've healed gunshot victims before. I hold my hand over the chest wound first but nothing happens. I shake my hand and hold it over again. My eyes squeeze tight in concentration, focusing on the task at hand and willing my light to respond. Malakai paces the surrounding area. It's only a matter of time before a shade arrives. A small short spark ignites but the light immediately turns off.

My mind races. Am I missing something? This is the mayor. Hell, he just came from a charity event. He's got 'good man' written all over him.

"What the hell? Help me out here dog."

"I haven't seen this before. Are you doing it right?"

I hover my hand over the top of his bullet wounds, alternating between his chest and abdomen and still nothing happens. "It's not fucking working." His breathing alters, becoming short and choppy. Outside air is filling into his chest, creating a pneumothorax. I need to seal off the wound and hope that he can breathe off the excess. "Shit. We're losing him."

I rip off my jacket and shirt. The shirt I lay on his chest, using my belt to hold it tight over the wound. "We need to get him to a hospital."

"How do you propose we do that? I can't help you carry him and you're not allowed inside of a hospital."

I grab the mayor's arms and pull them both over my shoulders, heaving him up and onto my back. "I'll carry him. Just keep the way clear."

Malakai trots out in front and I stumble along behind, tripping a few times, dropping him a few more, but I manage to keep moving. Unsure of the extent of his internal injuries, time is not on our side.

We finally hit the pizza joint next to the hospital and I sling him off my shoulders and onto the sidewalk. I call Malakai over. "Alright, I need you to run to the front of the hospital and cause enough commotion to get someone's attention. Do this and I'll buy you as much pizza as your stomach will hold."

He runs to the entrance and jumps up at the door, howling and barking. He repeatedly pushes at the door, and for a second I think he's about to burst through the entrance. In the midst of Malakai's created chaos, I continue to work on the mayor's wounds.

The seal created by my blood-stained shirt seems to be holding. His breath becomes less erratic. I roll him over and see an exit wound from the abdominal wound. That means a bullet is still in his chest but the abdominal shot made a clean escape. There's a significant amount of blood but as long as his internal organs are positioned the same as every other human, no major organs were hit.

Finally, someone from inside the hospital makes their way to the door where Malakai is barking. A young woman pushes the door open and points her arm outward. "Aww, look it's a dog. I love dogs. He's so handsome. I'm going to get my phone and post a pic to Instagram."

Malakai bends down into a play position and runs toward me, turns, and races back to the young girl. Thankfully, she takes the bait and follows enough to see me bent over the mayor.

"What are you doing to that man. Back off. I'll call the police."

I'm sure this looks suspicious since I'm drenched in the mayor's blood by this point. "Ma'am I need you to get someone to come take this man into the ICU immediately. He's been shot twice and has a pneumothorax and some internal hemorrhaging. If we don't start a blood transfusion and get a chest tube in him, he will die."

She pauses. "Who did you say you were, again?"

"Ma'am, this is the mayor. Go get some fucking help!"

That seemed to snap her out of her trance. She runs back inside and in a few minutes, I'm surrounded by hospital employees who are loading him up on a stretcher and racing him inside. My heart pounds with excitement. This is what I craved in my past life, that moment of uncertainty, where any decision made could be life or death. I remember it gave me the best high, better than any drug I've ever smoked. The high of pure power, where I got to play 'God'.

Now, all I can do is sit back and watch. I'm completely powerless. I'm worthless, a man trapped in purgatory meant to work and my only ability for said work has been stripped away from me. This must be some sick joke. The 'Big Man's' way of getting back at me.

They wheel him away and I know I must make myself scarce before anyone starts asking questions about how the mayor ended up in his current state. There were only five witnesses who would know I didn't shoot him. Two drove off in a getaway car, one is unconscious, and the other speaks 'dog'. I'm going to be avoiding the police for a while.

Chapter 16

For the first time since he showed his furry face in my apartment, I wake before Malakai. I would lick him awake but he'd probably like it. My body aches and I feel like I got hit by a truck that then proceeded to back up and run over me again. All the muscles in my legs are taught and knotted. I stretch and hit the wall on the way to the kitchen. My stomach rumbles but for once it's not related to a hangover. I'm jonesing for some diner food, but dare not show my face back at Angelina's Café. The overwhelming guilt from destroying innocent lives drowns me and is enough to keep me away.

Instead, I search my cabinets for sustenance. One shelf has little white grains scattered all over. I pick up a box of Minute rice and find a hole chewed through the bottom. At least the rats found something to snack on. In the bottom shelf of one cabinet sits a dusty cassette boombox, complete with AM/FM radio. It still contains all its batteries. I slip it under my arm. In the back of the pantry is a half-eaten box of Cheerios. I grab a bowl that hasn't been washed. Whatever was in there last has solidified to the sides, a kind of muddy brown substance. I pick it off with my finger and pour the cereal.

Inside the fridge, I'm hoping for grapefruit juice. Instead, there's beer and some milk. A quick shake of the carton of milk reveals chunks sloshing up against the sides. It doesn't pass the sniff test so back in the fridge it goes. I resort to enjoying my dry and stale cereal with a tall glass of fresh squeezed beer.

I return to the couch with my findings and switch on the boombox. With no cassette tapes to be found, I settle for radio static. Eventually a local news channel comes in over the airwaves with an update on the mayor's condition.

"Last night, after the annual charity gala at Spectrum Center, Mayor Poplar was brutally attacked and suffered two gunshot wounds. He was brought in to Blister City Medical by an anonymous individual.

I'm here with Mayor Poplar now. Mayor, can you tell me how much you remember about the events of last evening?"

"Thanks, Chelsea. I don't remember much. I remember getting in my car to go home and the next thing I know, I'm waking up in a hospital."

"Pretty scary. The doctors say you are lucky you survived."

"I don't think luck had anything to do with it. I don't believe in luck. But I do have whoever saved me to thank. If they are out there, I want them to know they have my full gratitude."

"I understand, Mayor, that you want to offer a financial reward to anyone who can offer information on the whereabouts of who helped you."

"That's right, Chelsea. My savior will, of course, receive an even larger reward. I am completely in their debt."

"Do you care to comment on the outcome of the charity gala itself?"

"It was a great success. There was a large turnout and we had a significant number of donations. I was going to wait to make a public announcement, but all the proceeds from the gala will be used to fund the new children's wing at Blister City Medical. Our children deserve the best care possible and now they will be able to

receive it right here in Blister City. We're hoping to offer discounts or free clinic days to our lower class citizens as well."

I smack the cardboard box that serves as my coffee table. The dry cereal flies in the air and scatters about the room. "Ha. I knew it. I fucking knew it."

Malakai sits up with the commotion. "Excuse me, sleeping here."

"Wake up and listen to this. The mayor's on."

"That sounds like a great proposal, Mayor Poplar. You've already done so much for Blister City, and I know I'm not the only person who's thankful someone was watching out for you last night."

"Thank you, Chelsea."

I click off the radio. "Unbelievable. Tell me how I'm supposed to achieve all my 'heals' in time if my own hand can't tell the difference between good and bad."

"You still lost me."

I point at the radio. "That reporter just interviewed the mayor. He's donating all this money to a new children's wing at the hospital. That donation right there makes him a 'good guy'. Think of all the kids he'll be helping."

Malakai yawns. "Look at you caring about helping people. What a good boy."

"How long have you been speaking to me like I'm the dog?"

"Long enough for you to have noticed before now."

I shrug. "It still doesn't explain why I couldn't heal him."

"He's a politician. They're always hiding something."

Malakai has kicked my ass to the light. Healing others is my calling just like it was before…before the accident. With most of the day in front of us, I decide not to waste it. Ginger should be home or working her cashier job. Time to take a chance.

Malakai jumps up to follow me. "Where are we going?"

"I need to fix things with my lady. You can stay here. I'll be back later."

"No deal. I've been instructed to follow you wherever you go."

"Fine. It's time to get you some real dog food, only the best Kibbles and Bits for you."

Parked outside her white front door stands a man with a plan and a fist full of fresh picked tulips he napped from the neighbor's front yard garden. If the door opens, she's going to slap me. Our last encounter was less than cordial. Perhaps a card left in her mailbox would have been the smarter approach. My finger taps the door to see if it's safe for knocking.

The door swings open unexpectedly and I'm left standing in front of the hottest grocery store checkout girl, the one where you'll wait behind four other customers just to let her handle your meat. It's that not over assuming polo shirt and khakis look, accessorized with a name tag and her hair done up in a ponytail. Her face dawns a scowl and the door swings shut. I reach my hand up to stop it. "Wait."

"For what?"

"There's no excuse for how I acted the other night. I'm dealing with some shit right now, but realize it was no reason to take it out on you." I offer up the flowers and hopefully sufficient 'doe eyes'.

She doesn't take them. "Look, I deal with dicks every day at work. I don't need them in my personal life as well. There're three kids I need to think about. This was all just a mistake."

"I respect that. I only came by to apologize."

"Good. Well, thank you. Now, I have a few errands to run and then work so I really must be going."

The door swings shut again and I reach out to stop her. "Can I walk you home tonight? Just so we can talk. I don't expect anything else."

Malakai shoves his nose between my legs and lets out a short bark.

"What's with the dog?"

"This is Malakai. He's my service animal."

A half-smile forms on her juicy red lips. "I always thought you were a little slow." She reaches her hand down for him to sniff and Malakai gives her a big wet lick. "He's sweet."

I look at Malakai and I give him the look of death. He puts on the charm by rubbing up against her and dancing back and forth with his feet while she continues to scratch him. Her shoulders drop and she looks like she's relaxing. This must be why they call them service dogs because he's getting me back into the action.

My hand extends once more. "You sure you don't want these flowers? They weren't easy to find." My hand extends once more showing the roots attached to the end of the tulip bulbs, covered in soil.

She peaks around the corner and looks at the hole dug in her neighbor's garden. She shakes and takes the flowers. "I'm sure they were quite expensive."

"So, do you want to just call me when you get off work? You have my number, right?"

"Yeah, sure." She takes a sniff of the flowers. "I didn't want to mention anything, but I've been having trouble with one of my exs again."

"What do you mean, again?"

"He paid for a lap dance a few nights ago and now he keeps buying me things. I think he wants to get back together or something. I just get a weird vibe from him. He was very possessive before when we were together. I can't describe it. He just makes me uneasy."

"Can't you get a restraining order or something?"

"Not that simple for a girl with my profession in a town that doesn't care about its nightly citizens."

"What's he look like?"

"Your standard male who frequents a strip club. Good looking, blonde hair, about five-foot-ten, medium build. Dresses nice."

"Wait, this isn't GQ, is it? The suit I met the first night I walked you home?" I swear I'm going to pummel that guy.

"I don't know who you saw. Last night he tried to wait for me by the exit. One of the girls gave me a warning so I slipped out the front, hoping he didn't see me."

"Well, I'll be there tonight so you won't have to worry about him anymore."

She smiles and closes the door. That smile is enough to give me chills. Every part of my body wants to burst back through that door, throw myself on top of her, and whisper sweet nothings all the long night through. But, I don't. Duty calls. Or at least a dog calls that has run off chasing a squirrel.

Chapter 17

Six hours 'til morning and twenty-eight days left. Tonic water with lime is my drink of the evening because sober drinks should taste like regret. The condensation beads up and drips from my glass, splattering onto the concrete below. I swirl the ice and liquid and tip the glass back, catching an ice cube between my teeth to crunch. Perched on a rooftop bar overlooking the city, I'm a man looking for danger. Malakai waits on the ground, pissing on fire hydrants and eating who knows what off of the ground.

This bar is on the nicer part of town. The rooftop is private elevator access only. It's the closest to uptown where I can still afford the drinks. There's a pool in one corner and a DJ in the other with small tables scattered between. My feet tread back and forth, restless and ready to get to work. The night is sweltering and not even a stray breeze offers relief. I roll my sleeves up to cool off my arms that are drenched underneath the leather. If nothing happens in the next thirty minutes, I'm joining the pool party. I really should consider some lighter attire in the heat of summer.

Standing a short distance away is a man dressed in a blue blazer with jeans and the same 'I don't give a shit' attitude that I see staring back at me in the mirror every morning when I wake to find I am still in purgatory. His eyes are watching the streets as well, just in the opposite direction. He pauses to take sidelong glances in my direction. I pull the sleeves back down to cover the scars. I get the impression he's checking me out. He points to his arms and nods. Out of all the bar patrons, he is the only other customer wearing long sleeves. I suspect he's hiding something as well. He's either a psychopath or one of my fellow healers.

I move closer to him and strike up a conversation. "Hot one tonight." I was always horrible at small talk.

He nods back but doesn't say anything. Clearly he's not a fan of mindless banter either.

I push up one of my sleeves to show him a feather shaped scar. "I think you and I share a common occupation."

He pushes up his blazer sleeve to show off his own battle scars. They're much different from my own. Instead, I see insect-like wings, like what you would see on a beetle or a fly. Those translucent, paper-thin wings that have deep ribs or veins running through them.

Does this guy have the same powers? Perhaps a little performance will determine what he is capable of. My hands wave in the air like I'm David Copperfield about to perform my latest trick of breaking and mending. I slide my left hand across the top of the railing, lift it up, and smack it down, catching one of my fingers at a bad angle. It's hard enough to break it, leaving a floppy digit. The man's still watching, his face unphased by my demonstration. I grab a cloth napkin off a nearby table and drap it over my injury for increased theatrics. Then, my right hand hovers over the left, heating up and emitting a soft glow. The pain disperses and the digit realigns. I rip the napkin away and reveal a now healed hand. Let's see him beat that.

He pulls a knife and I jump back. The blade turns toward himself, carving out flesh along the inside of his forearm.

Misjudged that one. He might actually be a psychopath. Blood flows and drips from the wound. His other hand remains at his side. Instead, he opens his mouth and a light pours from it. It shines over the flesh wound. The blood that drips down his arm sucks backward into his veins. Even the blood on the pavement rises in the air and returns to where it belongs. His skin seals shut until there's not even a speck of evidence that anything was disturbed.

He wins. Damn, even all the other freaks that I meet are cooler than me. His gift is also stronger but from a less convenient body part. Since the light comes from his mouth that must be the reason he isn't very chatty. I offer up my hand to shake in a truce.

All of a sudden, a siren echoes through the city. Below, Malakai darts back and forth. He lifts his head into the air and howls along like an idiot. A few blocks away in the direction the sirens are heading is a body lying on the sidewalk. I turn back to address the other healer to see if he's going to get this one or am I, but he's gone. I shrug. Looks like this one's mine.

My feet take the stairs two at a time. I reach the ground floor already huffing and wheezing. I really need to find a better way of getting around. Malakai meets me and we hit the streets running, somehow keeping a descent pace. Malakai holds back to match my stride.

We reach a four way stop. He looks up at me. "Which way?"

"I think just another block up and then to the left."

My muscles squeeze together into a cramp. I slow down and place a hand on my side. We hang a left and see the guy on the sidewalk. He's in his mid-seventies, bald and it looks like his glasses absorbed most of the fall. The frame's bent and the lens is shattered. I check for a pulse and find an erratic one. His color is pale and he has a faint blue hue about him. No shades yet, but I'm sure they're right on my heels. My right hand is behind my back, and I can feel heat. It knows this one needs saving.

My assessment is cardiac infarction, i.e. heart attack. We got here just in time. If I don't unblock the clogged artery and restore proper blood flow to his heart tissue, he may die.

My hand is placed directly on the man's chest, over his heart. Light pours and his pulse returns him to the land of the living as the rhythm normalizes. Color returns to his face as normal blood flow is restored. He takes a deep breath and sits up.

He rubs his dazed and glassy eyes while searching the ground for his glasses. Squinted eyes with a wrinkled brow stare up at Malakai and me hovering over him. He screams. We jump back. Then he scrambles to his feet and runs away.

I shout after him. "A simple 'thank you' would have been nice."

My back's on fire with the feel of bubbled flesh forming a new feather scar. "I met another healer up there on the roof."

"Oh, yeah?"

"His light flowed from his pie hole. He looked like he swallowed a firefly."

"That sounds interesting. Did he also have your chipper personality?"

"Hey, I think I'm growing on you. Just imagine what that guy has to deal with whenever he is forced to heal someone."

Things quiet down and we wander upon a residential area. There's a line of short bushes out in front of a row of houses. Malakai shoves his head into one of the bushes and pulls out a tennis ball. He keeps it in his mouth as we walk, repeatedly chewing and salivating on it, until there's a thick white foam that sticks to the fuzzy outer texture of the previously neon green tennis ball. A man with his arm in a cast pushing a red framed bicycle with a white seat approaches us from the other direction. He wears suspenders overtop of a pinstriped shirt. He looks strangely familiar. This is the hipster I wouldn't heal earlier.

Malakai stops directly in front of me. I come to an abrupt halt, almost falling over him. "What the hell, Malakai? Are you trying to take out my knees?"

His ears stand straight up and swivel. He drops the tennis ball. I pocket it for him. He lets out a small growl. "I hear something."

I quiet my breathing and listen more intently. There's the normal late-night sounds of the city, leaking pipes that drip, the low rumble of distant cars, and the electric sound of artificial lights that create the illusion of comfort in an otherwise frightening world. I'm about to tell him he's crazy when I make out the mumble of voices. It's soft, a few blocks away, but the short choppy nature of the voices makes me think of an argument that's escalating.

A scream rings out loud and true and that's our cue. Malakai turns to run but I stop him. There is no way I am running anymore tonight. The hipster with the bicycle is conveniently in front of me. "Give me your bike."

"No. I need it."

"You're not even riding it."

He lifts his arm in the air. "I will when my arm heals."

I ball my hand into a fist. "Don't make this difficult for you. Give me the bike."

"No."

My clenched fist reaches back and makes contact with the side of the man's face. He bends over to cradle his face and I rip the bike away from him.

I straddle the bike and look at Malakai. "Lead the way."

"Don't you want to heal that guy you just smacked?"

I look over my shoulder and see him sitting down on the ground. A bruise is already forming where I punched him. "No, he's fine."

Malakai runs off and I peddle after him. The wind whips past me and the air is a nice relief from the sweltering heat. We turn off down a back alleyway. Up ahead is a girl pinned against the wall. A man wearing a baseball cap pushes against her and shoves her backward, his hand covers her already bloodied mouth. She bites down. He cries out and retaliates by smashing her face into the wall. It's too much for me.

I skid the bike to a stop and jump off. My hand grabs the back of the man's collar and pulls him off her. His pants are unzipped and I pray I'm not too late. Malakai lets out a low growl and looks over to see if this one's mine or his. I nod and Malakai leaps in the air and knocks the man to the ground. His arms cover his face and Malakai snarls and snaps at his flesh. The man rolls away enough to make his escape down the street. Malakai gives chase, nipping at his heels the entire way.

The woman cowers in the corner. I approach her with my hands raised as a simple gesture that I'm only trying to help. I cover her bloodied mouth with my hand. She shivers with fright as tears mix with smeared blood into the brick imprint of this poor girl's face. I brush the side of her face and my hand sparks to life. Her eyes widen at the sight and she sinks her teeth into my hand. She screams. I startle backwards and her foot connects with my manhood. I collapse to the pavement and watch as she runs off in the other direction.

Chapter 18

Malakai returns to find me still rolling around in the dirt, cupping my nuts. "Did you find a good scent to roll in? Save some for me."

I cough. "She kicked me in the balls."

"Did you at least heal her first?"

"No. She bit me and ran away."

"My kind of woman. You know scaring them off before you heal them isn't ideal for business. Now get up."

I pick up my bike and delicately get back on. Ginger's shift is over in thirty minutes. One heal is enough for tonight. I peddle a little slower while we head in her direction so it doesn't look like I was waiting for her call. Desperate men do not get laid.

We waste time at the intersections of Graham and Sugar Creek. Malakai is sitting, sniffing the wind and his ears are perked, listening for any sign of distress. I peddle figure eight patterns into the asphalt, leaning into the turns.

Then, a horn blares, followed by tires screaming out into the night. Next comes the smash of metal colliding into metal at a high speed. A brief pause gives way to a screech and a bang. This is going to be a doozie.

I peddle fast down Graham. My feet slip and the bike waivers. I steady myself and keep my head down. Malakai runs full speed next to me. The smell of spilled gasoline hits us before we see the destruction.

My wheels crunch on broken glass spread across the pavement. I hop down from the bike and assess the situation before me. There are at least four cars involved. A Prius looks like it just came out of an impound lot, the entire front end flattened. There's a pickup truck with a dent that is facing the wrong direction. A Camry and an Escort are also involved. Cheap plastic is everywhere and it's hard to decide where to begin. Smoke rises from several smashed engines.

Near the Prius is a man that's been ejected and lies in an unnatural position in the center of the road. The Prius's missing windshield is scattered about with pieces sticking out of the man making him look like a porcupine. His car is mangled beyond repair and his body's headed in the same direction. I rush toward him and somehow, there's still a pulse. There is one shard sticking into his neck from an odd angle. I know that if it comes loose, the common carotid artery will sever causing him to bleed out in roughly twenty seconds. He needs me the most.

I work quickly, removing smaller pieces of glass with one hand and sealing his wounds with the other. My fingers grab the glass by his neck but I hesitate; Deja vu. When my light's on full blast, I slowly pull. Blood spurts, spraying me in the face. With my other hand I try to hold off his neck but the flow is too fast. Quickly, I reposition so that the light pouring out of me hits the pulsing artery. A seal forms and the bleeding stops. The skin closes up over top. I feel for a pulse. It's still there. Weak but at least he's alive. Several pieces of shrapnel are still embedded in his flesh but none near any major blood supply. I leave him to work on the next one.

The guy in the pickup isn't bleeding and I almost skip him. He can't turn his head and mumbles about not feeling his legs.

My light responds, repositioning crushed vertebrae to relieve pressure on his spinal cord. I drag him out of the vehicle and pull him to the side of the road and out of harm's way.

My phone rings and the caller ID reads 'Boo Thang'. Ginger must be getting off work now. My needs will have to wait. I let it ring and get back to the chaos.

Inside the Camry is a woman with minor injuries compared to the others. She has whiplash as well as a concussion from the airbag that was deployed. Nothing that some Ibuprofen with light magic to wash it down can't fix. I move her to the side of the road with the pickup truck guy. Drifting in and amongst the pileup are two separate smoky shadows. They float through the already empty vehicles, blindly searching for souls to steal. I need to hurry.

My phone buzzes again and I hit the button to send it to voicemail. My fingers type out a short text. *Saving lives here.* I hit send. Ginger will have to find someone else to walk her home. I'm in a race of soul saving. The flesh of my back singes into three more feather scars.

Malakai signals me toward the Escort. A darkness lingers and drifts toward the vehicle. A shade has found the scent. This vehicle has half of another car in its back seat. The driver is unconscious but relatively stable. The passenger, less so. She's slumped over and her mucus membranes are muddy in color. I yank on the passenger side door but it won't budge. The shade transforms into a bird-like shape, like a raven. It flies right through the door and sucks up into the passenger's nose. I take a deep breath and point my light directly at her, hoping it's enough to penetrate the door. Her mouth opens and the shadow raven emerges with a round glowing object. I'm too late. The door gives way and the shade flies away with his bounty. The woman's color fades to gray.

I redirect my attention to the driver of the Escort who's still alive. Blood is smeared all over the steering wheel. White fragments of teeth stand out against the crimson backdrop. His wrist hangs limp from his arm. As I mend his broken bones, the pain in his face disintegrates. The bleeding from his mouth stops. With what parts are found, I reassemble his mouth, piecing the shattered fragments of teeth back together again. Finally, a sigh of relief. That should be everyone.

Malakai dashes to the crushed Prius. He bounces up and down on his feet, barking each time his feet touch the ground. He whines and scratches at the back door.

"Malakai, leave it. I did that car first. We need to get out of here before the police come knocking."

Then I see it. The other shade rolls across the pavement toward the Prius, attracted to a soul that's still in the car. Malakai pauses. He perks his ears, tucks his tail between his legs and runs away from the car. The sky erupts with an explosion.

A wave of heat pushes me back. I lift my arm up to shield my eyes and stumble toward the Prius. The flames leap and dance, striking the car. There's so much smoke that I lose the shade. Then, I hear it; muffled screams. Trapped in the back seat are two small kids. Their small fists pound on the glass. They kick at the door. The crushed metal has jammed the doors shut and there's no escape.

The smoke from the fire sends me into a coughing frenzy but I push on. With feet braced on either side, I yank on the door. The heat from the handle sizzles my flesh. The little fists continue to pound away on the opposite side, begging for escape. I throw my jacket off and wrap it around my wrist. One swift punch and I'm through the glass.

The fire singes the hair on my arms as I blindly feel around. The first child, a small girl, reaches toward me. I scoop her up and hold her tight against my chest, shielding her from the flames. We rush to the side of the street a safe distance away. The girl cries and points at the car. Malakai sits with her as I race to grab her sibling.

Back at the car, a small boy pulls at his leg. His foot is twisted and jammed underneath the seat. He takes a breath and smoke fill his lungs. Whether it's from the fire or the shade, I have no way to tell. I drape my jacket around his head to shield him. My hand reaches out and runs back and forth over his leg. My eyes water and I can't see if it's working. His body goes limp. With my arms underneath his shoulders, I give him one swift pull. He falls back into me and we rush to safety.

His sister runs to meet us but Malakai pulls her back. My skin burns and feels as if acid is eating away at my flesh. Over my shoulder I see that I am literally on fire. I drop and roll across the ground to snuff out the flames. While still feeling like I've been served extra crispy, my hand points toward the boy's chest and his whole body glows. Smoke pushes out through his nostrils and he sits up and coughs. The sister runs to greet him and they embrace each other.

The human hedgehog Prius driver I worked on first is still laying in the middle of the street. The flames follow a gasoline trail toward him. I give him one more good heal and he stirs. He looks over and sees the flames overtaking his car. In a panic, he races toward it. I tackle him and try to explain that everything is okay. He fights me, kicking me in the ribs. I grab his face and turn it toward his children safely waiting on the sidewalk. His body relaxes and I help him over toward them.

I stand with Malakai from a short distance and watch the family reunion. There's hugging and many tears are shed by all. Malakai looks up at me. "Are you crying? Tell me you're not going soft?"

I rub out my eyes. "Irritation from the smoke. The dead don't cry."

"Ha. Right."

My phone buzzes and I reach into my pocket to retrieve it. This time I answer it but get nothing on the other end.

"What's up?" Malakai sees me staring at the phone.

"It was Ginger again but the other line was blank." I check the time and it's going on 3 am. Ginger's shift has been over for an hour. I better swing by her house and see if everything's okay. I put the phone away and stretch as more feather scars appear, these up and down my arms.

We arrive outside of Ginger's house. The lights are out and no body's home. If her shift ran late, she could still be at the club. I call her again. Straight to voicemail.

Chapter 19

I feel my tires grip the asphalt as the handlebar brakes are squeezed. There's an odd stillness to the night. The air's crisp causing the hair to stand on the back of my neck. Something doesn't feel right and Malakai can sense it too.

Where we should head straight, Malakai leads us left. We wander down a long back alleyway, weaving in and around the dumpsters. The ground is wet and water pools near a grate in the center of the road but it hasn't rained today. Drain pipes hang off the side of the buildings that line the alley. Water droplets splash down from the pipes and echo through the silence. Even in the darkness of night, the moon reflects off the bare brick walls, illuminating the scribbled graffiti of someone's claim to this piece of shit town. Then, I see them up ahead.

Up ahead, two silhouettes dance under a street light. They twirl together and then split apart. One crumbles to the ground. As I get closer, my eyes focus on the nightmare laid out before me. A man in a suit stands over a woman in a dress with red hair who's lying in the street. She rolls to her side with her legs hunched up in the fetal position, hugging her abdomen. My eyes hone in on the sheen of the crimson that drips off the tip of the knife that the man in the suit holds.

The bike's collapse is only a second before my own. I crawl on my knees over to her. Ginger's head is cradled in my lap and I brush her hair out of her face. She struggles to speak and I struggle as well.

The suit stands there watching us, frozen in time. I gently lay Ginger's head back down on the ground and stand to face him. He drops the knife and starts to back away. Ginger groans. I look down and see a separate blood source, a small trickle flows down between her legs. I crack my knuckles.

My fist connects with bony flesh. I feel the crunch of his nose breaking, blood pours from it until he chokes and gags on it. He swings back and somehow connects with the side of my face. He mutters something about it not being my business. I don't let him utter another word. I force him against a wall and slam my knee right into his nuts. He takes the defensive position and bends over to cradle himself. I brace the wall and kick his abdomen, again and again until his body drops and he's too still.

My chest heaves with adrenaline. The heel of my shoe pushes down on his neck, compressing his airway. Within arm's reach lays the knife, still coated in Ginger's blood. One good stab in the correct anatomical location and all this is over. Malakai barks in all the excitement. In my rage, I think he's cheering me on until I feel him pulling me back.

"Let him go, Scott. You can't kill him. He's had enough."

"You saw what he did. He needs to not exist."

"Let it go. If he recovers and has any sense, he'll never bother her again."

Ginger attempts to sit up. She wobbles and I rush to catch her as she falls back down. My lips kiss her forehead. The world has played a trick giving her beauty in one hand and men's contempt in the other. She's so radiant that someone tried to snuff her out. Under her hands, the wound is deep, blood seeping between her fingers. My hand lingers over the wound, testing it. We remain draped in darkness.

Her respirations increase, becoming shallow and erratic as her skin loses its color. She shivers, her body temperature dropping, sending her into shock. If I carry her to the hospital, we won't make it in time. My hand hovers above but there's no light to give. I use my t-shirt to apply direct pressure to the wound. In seconds the gray fabric becomes a sopping mess. I drape my jacket around her and pull her in close to my chest, using my body heat to keep us warm. With arms wrapped around her waist, I try to slow the flow of blood. I offer up a silent prayer that He'll do me this one favor, but I'm left sitting here alone with her life bleeding through my hands.

Her heart beats against my chest. Each beat is a reassurance that she is still with me. Each beat is longer until the next. She's lost too much blood and there's nothing more I can do for her except to hold her. I feel something drip onto my pants. It must be raining. I look up to the sky and see stars twinkling down, not a single cloud anywhere. It's then I half realize someone is crying.

Malakai walks over and licks my face. "Scott, we should get out of here."

"I'm not leaving her. She's a good person. It will work. I just need a minute." My fingers open and close and I strain my muscles, willing just a small spark to ignite from my hand. Still, my hand is cold.

"It's okay, Scott. Think of all the people you healed tonight. You dove into a burning car to save two children. You did good."

"Why didn't I answer my phnone? I would have left if I'd known. I would have been here."

"Scott, it was just her time."

"Oh, come on. You know that's fucked. Just leave me alone. Go on, git." I chuck a handful of loose stones at him. Malakai yips. "I'm done working for your god. What's the point in helping people if I can't save her?" I smack my hand against the pavement, pounding it over and over again. "Come on. Work. I know you have one more heal left in you."

Then, I feel it. My hand heats up, burning brighter until the light blazes from it. I direct it toward her wound. Her flesh sizzles. The wound closes from the inside out, growing smaller and smaller with each second until it seals closed. Her pulse is still threaded. All bleeding stops eventually but thankfully hers stopped just in time. She needs a transfusion. Stat.

I look for Malakai and he's still close enough. I call him over and run my fingers through his thick fluff. "You're still here. What a good boy. I need your help. We need to get her to a hospital."

Surprisingly, he doesn't have a smart-ass remark for me. I scoop Ginger into my arms and look at the bike. There is no way that's going to work. I sigh and jog in the direction of the hospital. This is the evening that just won't end. Malakai slows to let me catch up but I urge him on, hoping he gets there before me to cause a big enough disturbance.

We pass by the scene of the car crash from earlier. Police and firetrucks are still working to clean up the mess. Tow trucks load up and haul away the wreckage. The whole area is blocked off with traffic cones. Two ambulances with their flashing lights on are parked off to one side. This gives me an idea.

I whistle and Malakai runs back to my side. "Look boy, time for you to cause another commotion. That ambulance is the best chance we have of getting Ginger to the hospital in time. I'll never make it carrying her like this."

He runs off while I wait with Ginger. The backdoor to one of the ambulances is wide open. Two EMTs are attending to a victim lying on a gurney in the back of the vehicle. Malakai barks at the EMTs to get their attention. They ignore him. He reaches in and grabs a few supplies with his mouth and takes off. He bows into a play pose and one of the EMTs takes the bait, leaving his post. This is my cue.

I prop Ginger up against the sidewalk near the smashed cars and run toward the ambulance in a panic screaming to draw the last EMT out. I carry on about missing how they missed one and that she was out jogging when she was struck by one of the cars involved in the accident. It sent her flying to the side of the road.

The other EMT returns and they discuss the logistics of both patients in the ambulance. They discuss how it could be possible that they missed a body. Thankfully they take the bait and place Ginger on a gurney and secure her in place. Time to split. I jump down and race toward darkness.

Chapter 20

Once hidden from view, I whistle for Malakai. He drops the supplies and scurries toward me. The doors close and the ambulance pulls away. I need to know that she is going to be okay. The entranceway barrier prevents me from being the one and Malakai would be thrown straight into the pound the second they'd see him running loose in the hospital. I need someone else to watch over her. Someone human. Someone who can stay with her for as long as it's needed because he has nowhere to be. Someone named Barry.

Crime scenes have a different appearance in the daylight. The bloodstains are cold, soaked into the sidewalk and soon to be washed away by the next rain or the street sweepers, whichever comes first. No police are present to investigate since I never reported the incident. If I ever see GQ again, I'll make sure Malakai is not around to stop me.

Malakai waits next to me. "Why are we back here?"

"I left the bike here last night."

Malakai sniffs the ground around us. "Well, it's gone now."

"Thanks, Lassie." I stand and we head north on Graham.

The normal swift percussion beats that can be heard two blocks from the 277 overpass have a scratchy sound today, a scuff tap. Barry still has his drumsticks but he's missing his bucket. His head is bowed and he's scratching the sticks across the concrete sidewalk in between strikes. The rhythm is dragging, not his normal upbeat tempo. He doesn't look up when I approach him.

"Where's your bucket?"

"The youth of this perverse city have relieved me of my only possession left in this world, my friend the bucket." He stops drumming and picks at a scab on his knee.

"Is that what's slowed your tempo?"

"That and I heard your lady friend met the wrong end of a knife. Such beauty should never be destroyed. Is she going to make it?"

"That's why I'm here. I need you to do me a favor, Barry."

He keeps picking at his scab. The flesh underneath is very pink, not quite healed. He pulls the scab off and the skin reopens. A single drop of blood bubbles up from his skin.

"You know that's never going to heal if you keep picking at it."

Barry nods and looks off into the distance. He hasn't looked me in the eyes once since I've been here. He's hiding something.

"Barry? Why won't you look at me? Stand up so I can search you."

"Search away. The only secrets I keep, I hide from myself."

"We'll see about that." I search him, reaching in and around his jacket. In the inside pocket, I find a plastic spoon. I hold it up so he can see it. "What the hell is this?"

"It's for eating."

"You didn't get this to melt down whatever you're hiding?"

"Most plastics have a lower melting point than any other organic material."

That much should have been obvious. Exhaustion is making me a little foggy. I don't need a fifth-grade science lesson from Barry to realize he's up to something. Plus, Barry is more resourceful than one would guess. I pocket the spoon. My search continues with him removing both shoes. He hides his typical stash of cash but it feels light, especially since I haven't visited Barry in two days. Malakai gives him the once over. Hidden under the cuff of his sock is a small clear plastic baggie containing a piece of folded up tinfoil. "Barry, this better not be what I think it is."

He still won't look at me. I unfold the foil and find a small amount of snow white. It's not enough to do any damage to a seasoned user but who knows if this is just leftover. I pocket the stash and keep patting him down, thankfully not finding anything else. No syringes in site and no track marks.

I shake my head. "So, what, I don't show up one night and you're already back chasing that dragon?"

"It was but a brief moment of weakness."

"Damn it, Barry. You've been sober for close to a year now. What the hell?"

"The greatest challenge is to hold your weakness in your hands and still be able to resist."

"Didn't anyone ever tell you that shit will kill you?"

"As a matter of fact, you did."

"Heh. Well, glad to see you're such a good listener." I finish patting him down and Barry holds his hand out, expecting payment. This time I don't give in. "If you agree to help me, I'll pay you after."

"Can I get an advance on my payment?"

"No."

"So, what is it you desire?"

"Ginger's hospitalized at Blister City Medical. She'll be there several days, possibly up to a week. I'm not allowed back through those doors for too many reasons."

"I shall watch over her as I would my best stash."

"Think you can handle that?"

"With the voice in the sky as my witness, this duty I accept."

I take another look at Barry. His skin is covered in a gray ashy grime, at least four layers thick. He has more hair on his face than on the top of his head. His clothes have fewer holes than mine but there's a stench of the gritty underpass that sticks to him. "We have to clean you up first. I'm afraid if I send you into that hospital looking like you do, they may try to admit you."

"I acquire only the best hypoallergenic of soaps for my most sensitive skin."

"You will use whatever I stole from my last hotel stay."

I tried having Barry live with me after I first healed him. Once he sobered up, he became antsy. He kept saying he wasn't meant to live in a cage. I figured he was so used to sleeping out in the open that he couldn't adjust to the sort of luxury he was offered. "You know you can always use my place. Even to crash for a few days. I'm hardly ever home."

Barry shakes his head. "Domestication is not for me. I tried it once but it made me itchy. The streets need me. Plus, I can't be your eyes and ears if I'm locked inside."

"Whatever. Just meet me at my apartment in an hour so I can get you cleaned up. You smell like the ass-end of a Somali refugee."

I turn the corner and walk a few blocks. Across the street, I see a man pushing a red framed bicycle. He's wearing a flannel shirt with a hoodie overtop. His arm is in a cast and a large bruise covers his left eye. I run straight for him screaming like a madman. He turns to see me and hands off the bike without any hesitation.

I push the bike toward home. The fingers of my left hand fiddle with the plastic baggie of Barry's stash in my pocket. Malakai trots ahead out of view. I pull out the bag and open the foil, hold it up to my nose, and take a long sniff. There's no sense letting it go to waste.

Chapter 21

Back at the apartment after a clean shave and shower, Barry can almost be mistaken for a proper gentleman; almost. I dress him in only the finest clothes the clearance rack of the nearest thrift store has to offer.

"You know, we could get you a job and let you try being a positive contributing member of society."

"What can be more positive than having a low carbon footprint?" Barry's in the kitchen opening and closing every cabinet I have. "Where would one acquire proper sustenance? I have a terrible case of the munchies."

I'm sure he does. "No sense in cooking for one. I typically eat out."

"Then let us venture out to fill this great void in my belly."

My stomach rumbles. Ginger is probably still in surgery so we wouldn't be able to get an update on her condition yet. "Okay. We eat first, and then you go straight to the hospital."

"Take me to a proper sit-down place with menus and waitresses so fine you forget about all your troubles for just a little while. Angelina's Café."

"I'll take you anywhere else in the city. Just not there."

"Why?"

"It's complicated."

After all the pain I caused the waitress and the life her daughter lives, growing up without a father because of me, the guilt is still too much for me to handle. I'm not ready to go back. I may never be. "Pick someplace else."

"I have chosen where I wish to break bread so you should uncomplicate things."

Malakai brings me my jacket. "They don't know it was you. Use this time to make amends and feed the poor."

The least I can do is keep an eye on them. I owe them that. I grab my things and open the door to shove Barry and Malakai outside. "Fine. We'll go to the stupid diner."

We head around the corner to Angelina's Café. Someone crashed their car into the sign out front. The pole's dented and all the lettering is now dark. The owner hasn't bothered to replace the sign yet and probably won't. It makes me smirk. I open the door for Barry and Malakai.

Barry hesitates and points to Malakai. "I'm pretty sure this temple of gluttony is for the two legged only."

"Temple? You must not eat here a lot."

I grab us a few menus and we head back to my open booth. It's always open. I'm amazed to see how this place stays in business. There are crumbs that litter the seats and I brush them to the stained carpet before sitting down. Barry slides in next to Malakai and I sit across them by myself. Barry picks up the menu and reads it like it's the most interesting thing he's ever seen, 'oohing' and 'ahhing' over every item. Malakai drools, long sticky gobs dripping from his tongue onto the table. I grab a few napkins from the dispenser and lay them on the table where the drool pools into a puddle.

Barry watches me. "Your furry companion looks almost hungrier than I am. Now, where's this tasty little waitress you keep talking about? She should not be denied the overwhelming pleasure of an introduction with one as dignified as myself."

I feel a hand brush up against my shoulder and I flinch. She sets an empty coffee cup down in front of me. "Hey there, stranger. Missed you."

My eyes focus on the table but the constant finger tapping belies my innocence. "I've been busy."

"I was afraid you found someplace else to eat. You brought a friend with today."

Barry stands and offers his hand. "The name is Bartholomew Winston Churchill the third. I'll have coffee for now when you get a chance."

"That's quite a name." She takes his hand and he kisses it. She blushes and smacks me on the back of my head. "Scott, you could benefit from some of your friend's charm."

I roll my eyes as Nancy leaves to fetch our drinks. I look at Barry with raised eyebrows. "Winston Churchill?"

"Yes?"

"I thought your last name was Jones?"

"Oh heck, I don't remember anymore."

There's a commotion in the back with the sound of crashing plates. A young girl's voice says, "No, Mom. Let me do it. I can do it."

From the kitchen emerges a young girl with blonde pigtails, carrying a large bowl of water. Her eyes are focused on the bowl and she takes small little shuffle steps. Her arms are extended and locked in place. The water sloshes over the sides. She pauses, letting the water settle before she continues her slow meticulous journey toward us.

She finally makes it to our booth and slides the bowl across the top of the table toward Malakai, the water still slopping over the sides. "Sorry, coffee's not ready yet."

Barry intercepts the bowl and leans over to take a sip. "Oh good. She supersized me."

Layla giggles. "That's for the dog, silly."

"Ah, I see. Even in here, they serve the dogs first."

I grab the bowl and slide it down to Malakai. "Layla, the animal is Barry and you already know Malakai."

Barry stands and bows. "How are you doing my fine young lady?"

She smiles. "Good. Hey, why haven't you been in here to see me? Mom said you used to come in here every day."

I can never admit to her my mistake. She doesn't even know what her life is missing or maybe by now, she does. "Work has been busy."

She raises her little eyebrows, questioning my employment status. I may dress the part of welfare check, but I earn my living. Always have. "Are you still going to ask my mom out on a date? She's been seeing this other guy, but I think I like you better."

"Who has she been seeing?" Good. A chance for stability in her life.

Layla sits down next to me. She grabs a napkin and folds it forwards and backwards, making a table setting. "Some guy. Grandma likes him because he's very important and popular. Some politic guy. He's okay I guess. But his hair is very bright."

There is only one person that comes to mind. "Is your Mom dating Mayor Jeff Poplar?"

"Yep. That's him."

"Huh. How did she even meet him?" Why the hell would a mayor date a waitress? Perhaps he has no ulterior motives. It seems like a weird political stunt to gain the public's approval.

"He comes here, usually when there aren't a lot of other people or he calls. He calls a lot. I was hoping that you'd ask her first. She's always liked you. But then you stopped coming so she said yes to him. He came over for a sleepover but had to sleep in Mommy's bed because he gets nightmares."

Nancy returns with a cup for Barry and sets it down in front of him. Like a good waitress, she fills our coffees to the top and leaves the pot. "I see my daughter has found you. She's been talking about that dog nonstop since you were last here. I can put her back to work if she's bothering you."

"She's fine." I blow off the steam and take a long drag, savoring the hot liquid that coats my insides. She fills it back to the top.

"What'll it be then?"

Barry chimes in first. "I'll have the most expensive and largest portion item that comes on the menu." He jabs me in the shoulder. "Scott here owes me a nice meal."

"One super deluxe breakfast combo coming in at a hefty $9.99. And for you and the dog?" She squeezes my hand. This time I don't flinch. "Just bring me your special and the same for him." I wink at her and she smiles and walks away.

Barry looks at me with his mouth open. "Another wasted opportunity"

"What?"

"In my younger days, I would have serenaded that woman to the moon and back."

"You heard Layla. She's dating the mayor."

Layla ignores our conversation to grab my jacket and pull up the sleeves to look at my scars. "You have more this time."

I pull the sleeves back down. "Yes, I do."

"I know they're magic scars."

"Do you now?"

I roll up my sleeves and show her one of the scars. No one besides Ginger has ever touched these scars. She runs her finger around the inside and then up along the middle of the scar, tracing the complete outline. Her touch is gentle, light, barely touching the surface. A faint glow follows her finger, illuminating every inch her finger traces.

Nancy approaches with our food as Layla finishes tracing the outline. "Layla, stop that. I'm so sorry. She isn't usually like this."

I cover my arms back up. "It's alright."

We dig into the food, all of us eating in silence, shoving our faces full of food as fast as possible. I mop up the extra egg yolk from my fried eggs with folded toast. Malakai licks his plate clean. Barry carefully cuts each pancake with a fork and knife into bite size morsels before placing each piece one by one into his mouth. Malakai and I watch, long finished with our plates, as Barry continues his marathon meal.

Nancy brings a second pot of coffee as I drink four cups myself. The caffeine courses through my veins making my hands shake. I need to crash. Barry finally finishes his meal and we say our goodbyes to the waitress and her apprentice. As the hot sun bakes our flesh outside the diner, I give Barry specific instructions.

"I need details. Ginger's status, what was done, all of it. You're old enough to be her father so use that. They won't speak with you unless you're an immediate relative. Use all the knowledge that you accumulated from doing drugs over the years to pretend like you know something about medicine. That way, the doctors are more likely to speak to you directly and not sugar coat it."

Barry nods. "I will not fail you. You'll hear from me when I have news to share."

"Thanks, Barry. You're a lifesaver."

"No, Scott. I think you are."

Chapter 22

It's been several hours and no word from Barry. Like a caged zoo animal, my feet leave a track in the carpet from pacing the same path in the apartment. Too much boredom is making me batty as I continue the same routine: take a lap, check phone, take a lap, check window, take a lap, take a leak out of said window because toilet is clogged, take a lap, check door. Repeat. Once I popped down to the quick mart below to borrow their phone to call my phone to make sure it still worked. It does.

Malakai grew bored of watching me and has since lied down to take a nap. I still haven't slept. No sleep until I know she's okay. He lifts his head and watches me pass by him for the thousandth time. "You're prowling the apartment like a cat and I hate cats. Quit before I chase you up a tree."

"What if she didn't make it and they just haven't told him yet?"

"Well, then she'd be dead and there would be nothing to worry about. You healed her enough to keep her alive. Take a nap. Or, we could dig you a cave. Caves keep me calm."

This must be a challenge from 'Him'. He allowed me to heal Ginger, but her life will hang in the balance until I can clock in a few more heals. If I got paid to work in the day, I'd think about picking up some extra shifts.

I check the clock and it reads 8:45 pm. Close enough. In the kitchen I grab the largest steak knife and sink it, handle deep, into the flesh of my thigh. One rotation to the right and I rip the knife back out. Blood spurts and oozes from the wound. It feels as if every individual muscle fiber in my leg was shredded. My right hand drifts over the wound and light shoots from it, sizzling the fresh and cauterizing the wound instantly. The smell of burnt flesh fills the apartment. The cells of my body accelerate, multiplying and dividing to repair the wound until not even a scar remains.

"You should be committed."

"You have your ways of waking up. I have mine."

"Fair enough."

I grab my jacket and head for the door. Malakai jumps up to follow me. "Where are we going? Are we going for a car ride?"

"Sure."

"Really?"

"Since when do I own a car? It's time to get back to work."

"That's the spirit."

Down the stairs to hop on a bike with nowhere to go. The tires jump the curve up onto the sidewalk. An hour passes, maybe more. We keep circling the same three blocks. Finally, a siren cries out. The release of adrenaline jacks my heart rate. This is the high I need. I'll smother myself in work and then I won't have to think of Ginger.

Flashing lights come from everywhere. They converge and travel block after block, taking me farther from my apartment than I have in years, possibly a lifetime. In the distance is an old movie theater. The place has been gutted and changed into a concert venue. A large crowd forms near the entrance. The guys are dressed in tight black vintage t-shirts that contain every band name plastered across the front from the Ramones to the Smiths. The girls are dressed in loose tops with cutoff jean shorts where the inside pocket hangs lower than the frayed end of the shorts. Their hair illustrates all the colors of the neon highlighter rainbow. This is where the ambulance pulls to a stop.

I ditch the bike and rush straight for the crowd. There are so many people gathered around it's hard to get my bearings. A small compact car is smashed. It looks like it ran up the sidewalk before colliding straight into a traffic light pole. The pole is cracked and the front of the car is bent around it from the impact. A trail of bodies lays across the sidewalk, following in the wake. I grab one of the bystanders to shake lose some more information.

With eyes as wide as saucers, he points at the trail left by the car. "This guy came out of nowhere. He just didn't stop… didn't stop."

He turns around and I see a large piece of glass sticking out of the back of his neck. I reach my hand up and heal him before he can turn around. The glass falls to the pavement.

I turn to Malakai. "Go do dog things and find whoever the ambulance isn't working on."

He weaves in and out of the crowd with his nose peeled to the ground and ears pinned to the back of his head. He pauses next to a man that is pulling himself across the sidewalk with a compound fracture. Bone sticks straight out from his leg, shattered to the point that even the marrow is visible. His clothes are tattered but he may just be dressed for the concert. At least four or five of the injured don't look like they could afford the medical bills that await them. This is my chance to score some major points for Ginger's sake.

I set to work on the compound fracture. The guy watches the light and his face loses all color as the light forces the bone back into place and the opening closes. His eyes roll back into his head and he passes out. No awkward questions. Why can't all my patients be so pleasant?

I point up ahead at a young girl lying in the street with a face for the big screen. "Go check on her while I finish up with this guy."

Malakai bolts toward her. A man approaches the girl from the opposite direction. He's wearing a blue blazer and jeans and looks familiar. Malakai grabs the girl by the collar of her shirt and drags her toward me. The man pushes him away. He kneels down over her and feels for a pulse. Then there is a lean into a kiss, full on open-mouthed tonsil hockey style. As he pulls away from her, a bright light shines from his mouth and he blows it over her chest. The light fades and dies off. She begins to stir. Looking at me, there is a faint head nod. I guess his gift is a good way to pick up chicks.

Malakai returns to my side and we weave in and around the spectators. We make it to the car and see the driver with his head pressed into the steering wheel of the car. A vulture lands on the hood of the car. It turns toward us and I see it has no distinguishing features. It's wispy and black, draped in darkness. I hear a faint whisper in the distance. *Mine.* With its head lowered, it bobs toward the driver, pecking at him like it's ripping his flesh apart. A ball of light rises from the driver and the vulture swallows it down. It's too late for me to save him. The shade has claimed another victim.

My phone buzzes. I check the number and it's Barry texting me. He says to meet him out front and that he has a surprise for me. This can only be good news. He wouldn't text if it was bad news. That's not Barry's way.

I look around. The ambulance and Mr Mouth are attending to the rest of the victims. My work is done here. We flee the scene of chaos and slip into the night. I hear sizzling and feel the burning of flesh. I take my jacket off to see several more feather scars appearing, my right arm now completely covered in scars. I grab the bike.

Malakai looks at my arm. "Keep it up and you may actually reach your quota."

As I ride toward the hospital, a strange thought forms. For seven years I've been in a sea of monotony searching for a way out. Now that I have a chance for change, a part of me hopes that I fail so I'm stuck here. Healing others and working towards my goal is the one thing that could strip me away from Ginger forever.

We wait out front and finally I see them coming towards me. She has her arm draped around Barry but she looks sickly and beautiful all at the same time. Her cheeks are filled with a pink hue instead of the ghostly white skin from before. She's wearing one of those hospital gift shop t-shirts that says 'I Beat Cancer' and it hangs loosely over her frame. A plastic barcode hospital band sits on her wrist. Her hair is stuck to her face and hangs limp, absent of its usual bounce. She sees me waiting outside and smiles.

Barry hands her off to me. "I believe you've been looking for this?"

I take her in my arms and give her a long deep kiss. "I'm sorry I let this happen. I should have been there."

She runs her hands up the inside of my jacket. "Barry told me what you did for me and what you are. Let me guess, you couldn't bear to let me go without one more lap dance?"

"Oh, I want all the extras with a discount of course on account of saving your life."

She drapes her arm around me and kisses my cheek. "I may be able to cut you a deal. What happened to James?"

"Let's just say he won't be coming around anymore."

I hug her and turn to address Barry. "How did you get her out so quickly?"

"This one's strong. A few bags of blood and rest was all she needed to get her back on her feet. The doctors wanted to keep her for observation since they couldn't understand her degree of blood loss without any external wounds. I assured them we'd come back in for a recheck. The front desk was more concerned about the bill than anything else or we would have been out of there faster. It struck me that some of the money I have hidden away would cover the rest."

"How do you have cash? I frisk you almost every day."

"I have a secret spot you have yet to find."

Malakai looks up at me and wags his tail. "Don't look at me, I sniffed his butt."

"The spot is my bank account."

I look at him dumbfounded. "You mean to tell me you have a bank account and have been living on the streets all this time."

"The money is from my old life before you healed me. I had a job, a wife, and a great salary with benefits. The wife didn't like the drugs so she threw me out. After you healed me and I got my life back together, I went to her to apologize. She had moved on. She looked happy. So, I left it alone."

"I'm sorry, Barry. I had no idea."

"What's there to be sorry about? You saved my life. Thanks to our little arrangement, I stay clean."

"I'll pay you back for however much her medical bills cost in full. It will just take some time with my current salary of a hundred bucks a day, but I'll pay you back in full. For the next few days, I will let you keep at least fifty percent of your earnings from working the streets."

"One hundred dollars a day? I make more than that in interest!" Barry bends down and places his hands on the asphalt.

"The city is calling me back to my post. Take care of my new lady friend here."

Ginger walks over and hugs Barry to thank him again. I look down at Malakai. "I told you I needed a raise."

"He pays you what you are faithful and just to handle"

"You mean…I'm being…Barryed?"

Chapter 23

The next three weeks roll by and I spend more time with Ginger than not. When I'm not with her, I heal. Barry continues providing intel on big public events. Where there's large gatherings of people, there's trouble. Both of my arms are now fully covered in feather shaped scars. A few bare areas remain on my back and chest but I'm starting to look insane. I can't remember my last binge night, not that I ever could. I'm in the best shape of my second life due to sobriety and a large amount of cardio from all the hours logged on the bike and my daily sexcapades. Ginger and happiness look good on me.

Ginger's still grinding the pole as well as working the cashier job. We argued for several nights about the dangers of being attacked again. She argues the attack was on the way home, not while stripping. There are only so many jobs for a woman with her talents, well one really. We don't discuss our pasts. She has her secrets, and I have mine.

Still, I don't trust assholes. When I'm not available to walk her home, I've paid one of the bouncers all of my previous drinking budget, $75 a day, to walk her home.

I also don't trust blissful serenity. This is supposed to be my punishment. Malakai says it's the 'Almighty's' way of rewarding me for healing so many people. I keep telling him the contentment in my old life led to a mistake that cost me my life. Seven days left and then what happens? If I secure enough heals what happens to Ginger? If I don't, then what happens to me?

This morning, Ginger is working her cashier job and the kids are at school. Malakai's hungry and I'm bored so we take a stroll to stretch our legs. We make our way to our favorite café.

A new sign's out front is fully functional. Quite a change from what I'm used to. I push open the door and a bell rings, announcing my presence. The walls have been repainted a robin's egg blue. The seats look like they've been refinished. I rub my hand over one of the countertops and it's smooth, no more sticky substance or greasy slime. The biggest change is people. The place is hoppin'. Tables are occupied and customers are smiling like they might actually be enjoying their dining experience.

Nancy greets us at the door and smiles. "We're slammed but your booth is still open. I always try to leave it open in case you drop by."

"What the hell happened? It looks like HGTV vomited in here."

"Do you like it?"

"No."

She smacks me on the shoulder and I slide into my seat. "I think it's nice. Jeff ordered the city to give us a grant to spruce up the place. He said it could help with business."

"Jeff?"

"The mayor. You knew we were dating, right?"

"Layla mentioned something. The place was fine the way it was."

"Let's be real, it was kind of a dive before."

"Exactly. It's a diner. That's the point."

"I'll go get you a coffee. Or, do you want a Latte or Frappuccino? Jeff got us one of those fancy coffee makers."

"If you bring me anything other than straight black coffee, I'm done coming here."

The place has an overall unfamiliar smell; clean. All the lights have been replaced and are now blazing bright causing me to squint. Soft rock music ballads play in the background. Even the carpet's new. The whole chipperness of the joint gives me a headache.

Nancy returns with my coffee and water for Malakai. I ask where her little assistant is today and just then I see the blonde pigtails skipping toward us holding a placemat and a box of crayons. I place our orders and Nancy moves onto the next table. Layla sits next to us and doodles away on the placemat. Her smile is infectious even with two teeth missing.

"There's something different about you."

She points at her mouth. "I lost some teeth. Jeff gave me five dollars for each one."

"Don't you mean the Tooth Fairy?"

"I'm too old to believe in that." She slides over the placemat. "Here I drew you a picture."

Before me is the most magnificent piece of art ever created by seven-year-old hands. There are four people and a dog all scribbled in immaculate stick figure detail. The one that looks like a human chicken with mange I take to be me. Next to the dog is a smaller figure with a cape. The remaining two are a woman standing off to the side and a man laying sideways next to me. There's a small squiggle next to the man's head.

She reaches over and interprets her piece of art. "That's you with your feathers and Mommy and me and Malakai. We're superheroes."

"Who's this other person?"

"That's a guy you beat up."

"How come Jeff's not in the picture?"

"He's giving a speech across town."

"So, do you see a lot of this Jeff fellow?"

"Yeah. He likes sleepovers. We stay at his place too. It's huge. His bedroom is bigger than our whole apartment."

"I believe it." I take a sip of coffee.

The waitress returns with our food. She sets a plate of Belgian waffles dripping in butter and maple syrup with a side of sausage links down in front of me. Malakai gets scrambled eggs and toast. "What are you guys talking about?"

I cut off a square of waffle, the crisp but spongy dough soaking up the syrup so it drips down my chin as I take a bite. "Layla was just telling us how large the mayor's house is."

"It's practically a mansion. I never visited such a nice place before." She wipes her hands off on her apron and goes back to the counter.

"He's got this really big shower in his bathroom too. He lets me use it when Mommy's working late and doesn't make it home for bedtime."

Malakai gobbles down his plate and Layla watches him. "Sometimes Jeff helps me while I shower."

I cut off a piece of sausage and take a bite. "What do you mean by that?"

"He says he just helps me because I don't know how to do it right yet."

I set down my utensils. "Layla, this is important. Does Jeff do anything that makes you feel weird? Does he touch you?"

Malakai licks the young girl's face and I can tell that he and I are thinking the same thing. She is the example of inno-cence. I clench my hands into a fist. I could fucking kill this Jeff. I'm afraid to ask any more questions but I force myself to continue. "Layla, does he do anything else with you when your Mom isn't around?"

"Not really. He works a lot. We did play photo shoot the other day when Mommy was getting her hair cut."

I'm up and out of my seat before she says another word. "Malakai, stay with the girl. I need to have a chat with her mother."

I bust through the swing door to enter the kitchen and see Nancy grabbing a few containers of dipping sauce for one of her plates. "Nancy, we need to talk in private. Now. Outside."

"I'm in the middle of my shift, Scott."

"I don't care. Take a smoke break."

"But I don't…"

I grab her arm and lead her outside. There's an overflowing dumpster and the smell of rotting spoiled food fills the air. Flies buzz and linger over the trash. I step on an egg shell and feel it crunch beneath my foot.

"Jeez, Scott. What is wrong with you?"

"End it with the mayor. Now. If he gives you any problems, call the police. Move. Get as far away from the bastard as possible."

"What?"

"Don't make me repeat myself. Break up with the mayor."

"Is this some sort of jealousy act?"

"Did you know he's a fucking pedophile?"

She folds her arms and looks away. "How dare you. That is not something to joke about."

I grab her shoulders so she faces me and look her directly in the eyes. "The mayor is doing things with your daughter, Layla. To what extent? I'm not sure. It all makes sense now though. That's why my light wouldn't heal him. He's a fucking pervert. I should have left him to rot in that ditch where he belongs." I clench my jaw and I can feel my face turning seven shades of red.

She stares back at me for what feels like a minute, like she's mulling over the idea in her head. "…your light?" She looks down at the ground and then back at me. "Never mind. Look,

Scott, I know you've always had a thing for me but this is not the way to go about it. Jeff is a good man."

"I'm sure he is, but that doesn't mean he's not a pervert. We all have secrets. His just happens to be touching kids."

"How can you even make that sort of accusation? Jeff is great with Layla. He never once did anything that made me question his intentions. I trust him with her."

"You shouldn't."

"I think I would know if someone was molesting my own child."

"Not if they're careful about it." I hand her my phone. "Call him now. Break up with him. Make sure you tell him to stay the fuck away from both of you or I'll personally make him regret he ever met you."

"Scott, I want you to leave. Go get that dog of yours and leave. Don't come back here. I don't want you around my daughter."

"What the fuck did I do? I'm not the one you should be protecting her from."

"I won't have you making up lies to get your way with me. And you certainly won't tell me what to do. I'm happy. Layla's happy. This is the closest thing she's had to a father figure since her real dad died."

That one landed deeper than she could ever know. "Fine. I'll leave." I open the door and whistle for Malakai who comes running toward us. "Don't say I didn't warn you. If you want to let some asshole touch your daughter, that's on you. Not me."

Her hand flies up and I feel the sting of her hand smacking me across the face. I shake my head and turn away from her. "Let's go Malakai." I slam the door shut behind us.

Chapter 24

My hand sweeps across the stack of paper on my cardboard box kitchen table. Empty envelopes and old newspapers rain down onto the floor. A single cutout article stares up at me from the pile below. It's the old newspaper report from the night that I saved the mayor. I crumble it up and toss it in the sink. With the click of a Zippo, it ignites. The edges of the paper blacken and curl, folding onto itself as the flames engulf it. I watch his face burn.

Malakai stands back from a safe distance, constantly staring at the smoke detector. "Will you stop that before the world ending beeping from that thing on the ceiling starts? You're going to burn the place down."

"That's why it's in the sink." I turn on the faucet to put the last flickering flame out, the paper now thin flakes of ash.

"You warned her mother and that is all we can do. It's up to her to protect her daughter."

"What about your friend? God can stop this, right? Can't God give the guy an aneurysm or some debilitating disease? Or better yet, maybe the mayor gets mugged again and this time I don't save him."

"You know that's not how it works."

"Yeah, well it's fucking bullshit." My foot flies out and kicks through the wall. When I withdraw my foot, plaster crumbles down to the carpet, leaving a hole.

"Great. Let's destroy the apartment. Want me to piss on the walls as well? Will that make it better?"

"Be my guest."

Malakai trots over and cocks his leg, letting out a warm yellow stream that sprays and drips down the side of the wall to soak into the carpet. I grab a rag, scold him, and mop up the mess.

"See? You do care."

My back leans against the wall. "That girl has her whole life ahead of her. I had a much younger sister growing up." I pause. "If my father had ever touched her…well…I just can't imagine anything that awful."

Malakai comes to sit next to me. My fingers run through his coat. There has to be a way to get proof to report him to the police. If he's going after Layla, he's had others. These assholes are always repeat offenders.

"So what's the plan?"

"What do you mean? I thought you just said it was out of our hands and that we couldn't do anything about it?"

"Not us, but someone else?"

Barry. If anyone can hear voices in the night, it would be him. It's time we paid a visit to my dear homeless friend under the overpass.

The rata tat tat beat of sticks striking buckets is back and accompanies my march to meet Barry. He wears a pair of kids sunglasses with neon orange frames today as the sun shines fully behind him. There's an audience today. A few street walkers passing by pause to listen and drop a few bills in appreciation. He finishes his song and gets a few claps before the crowd disperses.

"Now I know how you make all that cash."

"Sweet music from the soul deserves recognition in the form of mulla. What can I do you for on this fine day?"

"Need another favor."

"Oh, yeah?"

"What can you tell me about the mayor? I need to know the dirty dirty. Can I get anything for $20 that would ruin his political career?"

He scratches at his face. "Hmmm. Now you're going down risky territory there. That's a public figure. He's protected."

"You mean by the wind or something?"

"No, I mean by body guards. I'm afraid his secrets are locked up tighter than the Mormon Vault. Why do you ask?"

"The night of the charity event, I had a run in with him. But something happened and I wasn't able to use my powers to heal him and had to take him to the hospital. I originally chalked it up to coincidence, but now I'm wondering if I wasn't supposed to help him."

"It is unwise to question the universe and its ways." He pulls an unwrapped half eaten Slim Jim from his back pocket. He picks a piece of lint off, blows on it, then offers me a bite. I decline.

"I want you to follow the mayor. Find the skeletons he has hiding around the city."

"Such a task may require payment upfront and the help of all my many friends of the rat and pigeon variety. I will become so loathsome in appearance and smell that he will be forced to ignore my presence."

"It's for Nancy from the diner. I owe them my life. Layla mentioned something that makes me think he's touching her."

"My future step daughter?" Barry's face drops all color until he's pasty white. He takes off his sunglasses and rubs at his eyes with the back of his hand. He tosses the remainder of the meat stick to Malakai.

"I tried to warn Nancy, but she doesn't believe me." I pick up one of the drumsticks and try to flip it for affect. Malakai yips as the stick travels off course and hits him.

"Then we shall make her believe you. I'll follow Layla."

"I can't risk you being seen by Nancy. She was pretty pissed when I left, even to the point where I won't be offered the special at the diner any time soon."

Barry stands and taps the side of his head with his finger. "The hospital then. I'll admit myself if I have to. Addicts go to repeat sources."

"I need you to catch him in the act. How does scrounging for methadone help?"

"Ah. I shall remain in the new wing where the children's section is. He frequented that place often whilst I was watching over Ginger. Here he will be and here he will not expect to be caught."

I pat him on the back. "Report back to me the second you find anything. We don't have a lot of time. Let's catch this sick sonofabitch."

Chapter 25

Thirty-six hours without a word from Barry. He knows to only contact me when he's found hard evidence. I prowl the streets at night and during the day, making sure to pass by the diner at least every few hours, but no mayor sightings yet. With just five days left, Malakai urges me on to log my last few heals.

Tonight, Malakai and I find ourselves in a rundown laundromat off Sugar Creek, located at the end of a blacked-out strip mall. I decide to wash my clothes because everything I own is crunchy stiff with dried blood, piss, or vomit. Most of the machines are broken and require a certain number of kicks before transitioning to the rinse cycle. I'm already on my fifth machine and my last 4 quarters after my first load. I blew through those suckers like an old lady at an Indian Casino slot machine. Except instead of the thrill of flashing lights and spinning dials, I get the pleasure of a half washed heap of clothes.

There's an older woman sitting in the corner, waiting for her clothes to dry. She's knitting a scarf or a blanket or a pair of socks. Her knotted arthritic fingers shake and fumble with the knitting needles. Her already wrinkled skin wrinkles more in frustration but still she works. A young woman, dressed in athletic gear with headphones is sorting her clothes on a table. She bobs her head to a beat only she can hear. Other than those two, Malakai and I are the only ones in here. He's laying down, curled at my feet. I'm seated at the back, my head leaning against the back wall with my eyes closed letting the whirl and tumble of the machines lull me to sleep.

I picture the mayor smiling and shaking hands at some campaign event. The crowd parts and I race towards him with a crowbar and smash his head in. The next image is him standing at a podium, giving a speech, when I burst through the crowd with a gun and shoot him square in the forehead. This is my way of making amends. I can save countless young girls from a fate worse than death by killing the mayor and everyone else who stands in my way.

A group of four Hispanic men walking into the laundromat jerks me awake. These men are all dressed similarly, wearing athletic jerseys, each barring the number thirteen. Like they just returned from spring break in Louisiana, they wear alternating blue and white beaded necklaces. Three of the four members are covered in tattoos, a mix of the number thirteen, the letters 'MS', devil horns, or simply the words 'Salvatrucha'. The youngest member doesn't have any tattoos. I assume he's fresh blood.

I nudge Malakai to wake him up. "MS-13, the most violent group of assholes in the city."

We're not the only ones watching them. The old lady knitting keeps looking up at them and pulls her purse closer to her side. The young athletic girl's eyes dart about the room. She gathers her clothes and shoves them back into her bag. She heads straight for the exit but one of the men notices her. He makes a scene, whistling and grabbing at his crotch. I'm on my feet and heading toward him before Malakai can stop me.

I put myself in between them. "I believe the young lady was on her way out. I suggest you let her pass."

He eyes me, looking up and down my scarred arms. "What if I say no?" He lifts his shirt to show he's packing.

My face is inches away from his. "Tonight is not the night to piss me off." I lean back and headbutt him in the forehead. A small trickle of blood flows down into my eyes, blurring my vision. He stumbles backward and draws his gun.

A car engine revs right outside. The front glass explodes as bullets whip through the place. One smacks into the cholo's shoulder in front of me. The whole place erupts into mayhem. I grab the girl and throw her to the ground. I lay on top of her, acting as a shield. The old woman at the front is already slumped over in her chair, she the brunt of one of the first bullets. All four gang members inside the laundromat have their guns drawn and they fire back, yelling at each other in Spanish. I hear the words '42nd Street'. Great.

Bullets continue to whizz past, one strikes my leg and another hits my shoulder. All four members hit the ground like sacks of rice. The girl beneath me is screaming as blood flows from my wounds and drips onto her. I turn my head to the side and use my light to seal the wound on my forehead. My vision clears as I blink away the blood. The engine revs another time and I hear the squeal of tires as the vehicle races off. The non-tattooed member limps and holds his leg. He raises his gun to fire two more shots in the general direction of the car. He falls to the ground.

I stay where I am another minute until I hear nothing but silence. Through the broken entryway, two shades in the shape of hyenas float in and dive to the ground, sifting back and forth as they hunt. They lean over one severely wounded gang member and appear to fight over him. The smaller one wins and rips at the man's throat. It then retreats with its claimed soul with little concern from me. I roll off of the girl and pat her down to check for any wounds. Her face is white with shock and red with my blood. Somehow, she made it out of there without a single wound. She dashes out of there with her phone at the ready, leaving her clothes behind.

My feet slip on the blood spread across the floor. The old lady has her head flopped over to the side and blood trickles from the corner of her mouth. The larger shade sees me and races toward her. I dive for the woman but the shade is faster. As it floats over her cold and empty corpse, I hear a faint cackle. Can a shadow mock you?.

Two of the gang members and the old woman have been claimed by shades. Near the dryer is the new recruit crawling away. The smaller shade toys with the man, nipping at his heels as he drags his wounded leg leaving a blood trail along the floor. Since this man's skin is flawless, there's still a chance he can change if I help him. I roll toward them and send a large blast of light toward them. The blast slams into the shade. It shrieks and flies away. I grab a hold of the recruit and wrestle him to the ground. He's fidgeting and trying to get away from me, yelling at me in Spanish that I don't understand. "Hold still, damn it. I'm trying to help you."

My knees press into his stomach to hold him down. My hand drifts over to the bullet wound in his leg. The light glows and heats up his flesh as the bullet slowly retracts. Muscle fascia weaves into each other and severed tendons reattach. The subcutaneous fat layer pulls over the top, leaving the skin to zip closed. I pull away in time to leave a scar as a reminder. His mouth drops open and he reaches for his gun. I kick it away. "No, you don't. Consider this a second chance. I'll be checking up on you and if I ever see you hanging with this crew again, I'll put a bullet back in your leg the same way I took it out. Comprende? Now, get the fuck out of here before the police show up."

He scrambles out from underneath me and takes off running. The last remaining gang member, the one I headbutted, is still alive. His shirt is soaked in blood. He rolls back and forth on the ground and moans. The larger shade still remains and it snakes across the ground, like it's searching for a scent.

I take a long look at this man. His facial features are similar to the man that I just healed, making him a relative. He's a seasoned member for sure, gang symbols inked across his flesh. I could test out my light and see if there's a chance it might work, but he's not worth my effort. This man I leave to feed the shade. I turn my back toward him and walk away. There's a scream followed by a whoosh. Then there's silence.

I whistle for Malakai and don't see him anywhere. Perhaps in all the commotion he found safety outside. I walk back to the back of the laundromat to collect my belongings. There, curled in the corner on top of my clean clothes, he lays. He has his left paw curled. He tries to stand, whimpers and collapses to the ground. I run my hands through his thick soft coat and they come back sticky and wet with red.

Chapter 26

I hold my hand over his wound. The bullet retracts and the wound seals over. His black fur bleaches white to mark his previous wound. He puts his leg down and bounds around. "Good as new. Now let's get the hell out of here."

We take a turn and head in the direction of the hospital. Malakai and I could use a break after the mess at the laundromat. This area of town is safer and we'll be ready if Barry does try to contact me.

Malakai stops to take a piss, lifting his leg on each one of the few trees planted to line the street. "Things got a little intense back there."

"Yeah, I wasn't expecting to be caught in a gang war between 42nd Street Little Criminals and their biggest rival MS-13. I think I earned some pizza slices, maybe even a whole pie."

"What about me?"

"You were found laying down on the job while I was battling evil spirits and gang thugs."

"Hey, I was mortally wounded."

"Fine. I'll give you my crust."

I emerge from the great Canyon Pizza a minute later with two huge slices of cheese pizza. The grease soaks through the cheap paper plate and the cheese hangs over the edge, dripping down the sides. We sit down on the edge of the sidewalk. I lift the slice and fold it in half before taking a large bite. The cheese burns the roof of my mouth but it tastes so good that I don't even care. Malakai takes the whole slice in his mouth and gnaws it, drool pouring out from all sides of his mouth.

My phone buzzes in my pocket and I pull it out. It's Barry, telling me to meet him out in front of the hospital. Thankfully, we're already here. I finish my slice and see Barry coming out through the front doors.

I throw my hand out. "Let's see it, Barry. Hopefully the video's good quality."

"Nothing yet."

"What the hell? Then why did you call me down here?"

"I'm close."

"This isn't horseshoes and hand grenades. Evidence Barry. I need it."

"I sit on a trail so fresh the shit pile's still steaming. He comes to the children's wing twice a day, usually early before and after official visiting hours. There's this young girl there with leukemia. Pretty little thing. She's sweet too, seeing her would even break your heart. He's taken a special liking to her. Brings her gifts."

"So, what is that going to prove? I need to lock him up, not win him a humanitarian award."

"Nurses talk of sponge baths and photo sessions. Things they have walked in on that may seem innocent. But if your theory is correct, perhaps not so innocent."

"That's just all heresy. I need hard proof."

"Perhaps a certain someone did a little tampering with one such gift of the stuffed bear family. Think nanny cam of the hospital variety."

"How did you plant the camera without getting caught?"

"The city has taught me to go unnoticed, to slip in and out of the cracks without making a noise. The city has also taught me how to sweet talk a certain nurse."

Hopefully he does something that will be enough to nail him. He's got to be one fucked up individual to go after a sick little girl.

"Keep going, Barry. Whatever you have to do. Just do it fast." I hand him a few dollars. "Here's some extra change, not that you need it, but grab a slice of pizza for yourself."

"Anticipate a call by tomorrow at the latest from yours truly."

Malakai and I head off in the direction of Ginger's house. I feel the warmth of the sun rising as it brings the start of another day. Just four days left. My lungs take in a deep breath, inhaling the thick smog of the city that catches in my throat, leaving a sticky film. The progress Barry is making is giving me hope. If I can't log enough heals in these next few days, perhaps I can at least stop a pervert. The realization that if I hadn't killed Layla's father, she wouldn't be in this predicament hangs over me. It's my job to protect her now to make amends for what I have done.

We're outside Ginger's house now and I give a quick three raps to her door. The most beautiful thing in the world answers the door. She's wearing only a towel and her red hair is soaked, hanging in wet tight curls that frame her hidden breasts. The towel dips down enough to squeeze her tits together, leaving a deep furrow of cleavage that I want to bury my head in. "I wasn't expecting you until later. Sorry, I just got out of the shower."

She steps to the side and lets us in the door. Malakai finds a couch and makes himself comfortable. I plant a kiss on her cheek. "We had a rough night and need to lay low to burn off the day."

She points at my bullet wound in my shoulder with the bullet still present. "I can see that. You want me to help you remove that."

I look over at the wound. "Huh. Guess I forgot about it. I got it." I reach over and use my light to extract the bullet. I smack the freshly healed wound with my bare hand. "See? Good as new."

"I don't ever think I'll get used to that."

I head over to the kitchen and start mixing a drink; whiskey ginger, the breakfast of champions. I whistle a random tune in my head.

Ginger watches me and cocks her head. "What's up with you?"

"What do you mean?"

"You don't seem the whistling type."

I take a sip of my drink before setting it down. She looks so good in that towel that I almost wish she'd stay in it; almost. I massage Ginger's shoulders. "I've got something big brewing. Barry is helping me to destroy a man's career. We're close."

She leans into my hands as I work all the knots out of her shoulders. My right-hand heats up just enough to relax and soothe her aching muscles. Her ass pushes against my crotch as she rocks her hips back and forth. She whispers. "That song? The one you were humming? You know that's my lap dance song, right?"

I press deeper into her shoulders and I thrust my erection into her hip. She groans beneath my touch. "I'm aware."

My fingers slip under the towel testing Ginger's response. Her bare skin is smooth and slick with fresh lotion applied. She smells like vanilla cake and I want to eat all of her. My fingers slide higher up the inside of her leg until I slip one finger in. She adjusts herself to allow me to enter her. She's warm and sticky wet; inviting. "I think I have that song recorded on my phone. I could play it for you as a private show?"

Two more of my fingers slip in and she gasps and pulls away from me. I bring my fingers up to my mouth and lick her off of me. "Whatever you want." I pull her in to kiss her, my tongue touching hers.

She drops her towel. "I think I just want you."

After we're both spent and satisfied, we retire to her bedroom to relax. The blinds are drawn, leaving us bathed in total darkness. Her naked body lies next to me fast asleep, breathing deep and slow. I drift in and out of sleep as the hours pass. I'm anxious to hear from Barry. I decide to go find my phone. I pull the sheet up to cover Ginger. It's hot so she doesn't need it for warmth but it gives her a sense of protection. I pull it down just enough to leave her fun bags out in the open. I don't want to wake her so I roll slowly and slip out of bed.

She hears me anyway. "Where are you going?"

"Nowhere. Just sleep."

She's read my mind. "You're going to check your phone. Let me know what time it is. I have to work tonight." She sits up and rubs the sleep from her eyes.

I head out into the living room. Malakai is stretched out on the couch, passed out on his back with all four of his feet in the air. I grab my jacket, crumbled on the floor in the entryway and find my phone jammed inside. I switch it on. It's 8 pm, another day wasted. No missed calls and no messages. So, I guess that means nothing to report, but my end is imminent and I can't keep waiting.

My mind keeps spinning the options. I pace over toward the living room. "Malakai? Wake up, buddy."

He spins off the couch so fast that he lands on the floor with a thud. He limps around and shakes himself off. "Robber? Robber?"

"Barry hasn't called yet. We need to split."

"To track him down?"

"Not yet. We'll give him one more day. The mayor probably was too busy to visit today. Do you want to sit this one out and rest that leg of yours?"

"Nah, I'm up now and have to take a piss. I'm just stiff." He turns and starts licking the gunshot wound site, cleaning the last bit of dried blood from his fur.

"Let me say goodbye to Ginger."

I walk back into the bedroom and see that Ginger is awake and changing. "It's 8 pm and I need to get going."

"I have to go to work soon anyway. Are you going to stop by the club tonight?"

"We'll see where the night takes me."

She takes me in her arms and gives me a deep kiss. "Go save the city."

Chapter 27

Malakai and I spend the entire night saving lives. Both arms and my entire back are now completely covered in overlapping feather shaped scars save for one small area on my right side. Just enough space remains for a single heal scar and I have three days left of my sentence to make it happen.

The city is flourishing with life the next morning. Street side vendors greet us and try to land us a deal on stolen watches, wallets, and sunglasses. Artists play music or sell hand drawn sketches to make a buck. All storefront shops are open and inviting. We stop at a corner newspaper stand and I grab a paper to keep the man in business. A cart vendor next to us is selling hot pretzels and I grab one as well. I rip pieces off the soft chewy salty dough and toss them to Malakai. With all the friendly faces about, I feel like I'm trapped in some dark version of a kid's animated feature. All I need is a talking animal companion and I'm set. Oh wait…

We reach the hospital entrance and there's no sign of Barry anywhere. I check my phone again; still no call or message. My watch says 10:30 am. I run my hands through my hair. He was fairly certain he'd have something by now.

Malakai watches me. "Do you want me to cause another disturbance to see if I can draw someone out? I have a giant dump saved up and if we wait long enough someone is sure to come in or out those doors."

"Let's wait just a little longer."

Malakai falls in beside me as we wander the block. As we get to the far end of the hospital near Canyon Pizza, he pauses. He lifts one of his paws and I watch him sniff the air. His tail is curled and sticking straight up in the air and not wagging. "I smell something."

"Yeah, pizza. You know I just fed you, right?"

He takes another sniff. "No. Something else."

Before I get another word in, he takes off down the alleyway between the hospital and Canyon pizza. I'm hesitant to leave the front of the building but curiosity gets the better of me and I take off after him.

He's near the corner of a dumpster reserved for medical waste. Leaning up against the side is a mound, covered by a blue tarp. Malakai takes another sniff and whines. He lays down and places his head on the mound. A dirty pair of sneakers peaks out underneath. I pick up a corner of the tarp and pull it away. Under that tarp is my worst nightmare. A man is slumped over, lying on his side, with his face turned away from us hugging a teddy bear. A tourniquet is hanging loose above his elbow and a small empty syringe lies next to his arm. I don't need to see his face to know it's Barry.

"No. No. Shit. No." I roll him over and feel for a pulse but get nothing. My fingers shove inside his mouth and I pry it open. His flesh is cold and the muscles of his face and jaw are already stiffening with rigor mortis. My hand hovers but remains dark. I give him a breath and start chest compressions. My vision blurs as my eyes feel with tears.

Malakai paws at my leg. "Scott, you can stop."

Floating high above us is a shade. This one's shaped like a giant raven with longer talons on its feet and a few features that make it appear almost human. A tongue darts out from its mouth and appears to lick its beak. It utters, 'all done' and then flaps away.

"Don't you fucking say it, Malakai." I press harder and faster over his heart, using my weight until I hear his ribs snap.

"He's gone, Scott. Let it go. There's nothing you can do for him now."

"I know he's fucking gone. The idiot OD'ed again and it's all my fault." I grab the syringe and chuck it as far away from Barry's corpse as possible.

Malakai comes over and licks my face. "He was an addict."

I close his eyelids. "I just don't believe it. Other addicts, sure, but not Barry. He was clean for over a year. We had a system. Here I thought he was helping to save an innocent girl when all he was doing was looking to score. He knew I wouldn't be around to stop him."

"Addiction is a disease. I'm sure he intended to help. Something he saw in the hospital could have set him off."

The Bear. I pick up the stuffed animal and find a zipper in the back. All there is to do is find a TV and hook it up. We'll see what pushed Barry over the edge. The bear feels hollow like it's been under stuffed. I unzip the back. Where there should be 3 cables, there is nothing. In the front where there should be a lens hidden in a bowtie, there's a gaping hole.

"Shit."

"What's wrong?"

"It's not here."

"What do you mean?"

"I mean, the bear's been tampered with. The camera's been ripped out."

"You don't think Barry could have removed it after he watched the footage?"

"No."

"It might explain what caused him to do this." Malakai nudges Barry's body.

"Barry would never burn me like that. We've known each other for over ten years. Even before all this."

"Then who?"

"I don't know. Go sniff it out Scooby Doo. Find me some clues." I extend the bear to him.

Malakai buries his nose deep inside the bear. "I smell Barry. But I don't know the other ones. It just smells like sick people and antiseptic."

Damn. Dead end. There's got to be something else. I give Barry one last good frisk. I find nothing. No hidden cash, no phone, nada. He's been picked dry. I send Malakai on a search of the area while I check the nearby dumpsters.

He sniffs the entire area but we don't find any of Barry's things. He trots over to where I threw the syringe and stops. His tail sticks straight up in the air and wags back and forth.

"Get away from that syringe, dumbass. You're going to hurt yourself."

"Give me a minute. I got something." He keeps sniffing it and uses his paw to roll the syringe. "There's another scent here besides, Barry. A stronger one."

"Do you have any way to track it?"

He smells around again but finds nothing else. "What do we do now?"

"I can't just leave him here by the dumpster. It's Barry. Why don't you try to draw someone out here? I'll hide so they don't think I was involved. We'll ditch the syringe so whoever finds him won't think he's just another junkie."

Malakai paws at the exit door and barks as I hide around the corner. A janitor throws open the door. "What's all this ruckus?"

Malakai continues to bark.

"I ain't got no food for you. Run along now. No dogs allowed inside."

I can see Malakai pulling on Barry's clothes, pulling him into view. He nudges Barry, then whines.

The janitor steps out to take a closer look. "Oh, shit. That guy looks dead. I'm going to go find someone quick. You stay here, dog. I'll try to help your friend."

The door closes and Malakai runs to me and we head off down a few streets in the direction of the 277 overpass. No drum beats or percussion solos greet us. Hidden away in the shadows is Barry's trusty bucket. He has a few trinkets tucked away, wrapped in an old sweatshirt full of holes. A set of keys, a picture of his wife from long ago, a few tokens of sobriety, and his drumsticks. I pick the sticks up and run my hands over them, feeling the splinters bite into my hands. The wood is chipped and rough, just like Barry's life. A sticky sap is smeared on the handle of each stick; a trick Barry once told me drummer's use to prevent the sticks from slipping. They are worn and full of personality. I slip them in my back pocket and cover them with my shirt.

I leave the rest of his belonging including the bucket to the streets as an honor to Barry. I look around one last time, then walk away.

Malakai follows. "So, what now? Do we head back to your place until sundown and then head back to work?"

"Nothing."

"What do you mean?"

"I mean that's it. I'm done. We have nothing on the mayor. I can't save Layla because her mother won't listen to me and there's no real evidence to avenge Barry's death."

"Scott, you are one heal away from getting out of here and moving on. You need to focus on the task at hand."

"Anytime I try to do something good, shit happens and people get hurt. I'm better off being stuck here. No more healing for me."

"But you enjoy helping people. You were a great doctor in your past life which is why you were chosen as a healer in this one. It's who you are."

"Not anymore. Look, go find another 'Healer' to look after or you can go back where you came from." I pause, looking left and right. I finally decide to head left in the direction of The Underground.

"Where are you going?"

"I'm going to get piss-faced drunk."

"How is that going to help?"

"I won't have to think about anything else besides what to drink next. My last three days here will be spent in a blissful blacked out bingefest."

"If you black out for three days, you'll wake up in Hell or worse."

"Bring it on."

Chapter 28

I've lost track of the number of drinks I've downed. It's somewhere between five and not enough. My whole body tingles with warmth as the alcohol pumps through my veins. I feel like my head is plunged underwater. The barkeep is dusting random jars filled with pickled blurry shapes. He smears the outside of the jars with his rag, rubbing off the inch-thick brown grime. Even with the outside of the jars clean, I still can't make out what floats inside. I stare down at my unidentified brown liquor and take a sniff. It smells like smoke and wet leather. There's a fly flipping and spinning in the liquid, trying not to drown itself. I scoop it out with my fingers and suck off the liquor from each finger.

I look up at the barkeep again and tip off of my chair, falling to the floor. From down here, the view is old cigarette butts and a liquid sludge composed of spilled alcohol and the brown spit of chewing tobacco. I raise up back onto my stool and hold onto the bar to steady myself.

There's a band on stage comprised of a guitarist, ukulele, drummer, and a singer that plays the tambourine. Some country group singing about women and all their problems. Each downs their own beverage during songs. They play the stage like they're playing Red Rocks Amphitheater but no one here is listening. They drink to sound better.

There's an older gentleman sitting next to me with a bald head and glasses. He's wearing a polo shirt, he doesn't belong in this sort of joint. He's got the shakes and the ice rattles in his glass as he attempts to lift the glass to his lips. He drinks to get rid of the shakes.

There's a younger guy, dressed in flannel. He must be in his twenties or something. He's flipping through his phone and muttering things under his breath as he downs a few canned beers. He drinks to forget a girl.

I pound the rest of my drink and signal to the barkeep to top me off again. This is not a place where they question the number of pours. He fills it to the top with brown mystery liquid number three. I stare at my hand, welcoming the upcoming days when I can no longer heal myself. My lips press to the glass as I slurp up my adult juice, allowing it to drip down onto the scratchy stubble of my chin. I sit with my jacket in my lap, wearing my gray t-shirt that's sporting a few extra holes these days. I drink to forget a friend. I drink to forget a life. I drink because I want to give up but I can't.

A black dog bursts through the door and runs up to me. He's soaking wet and shakes off, the splatter landing all over me. I go to stand to greet him and the room tilts so I sit back down. "Hey. Hey, dog. I know you."

He walks over and barks at me. He pulls on my pant leg and I swat him away. He sits and lets out a low growl.

I take another sip to keep my body buzzing. I look at the dog. "This is some strong stuff. I should get you one. Hey barkeep, get my furry friend a drink of whatever the hell this is." I tap the glass and take another sip, spilling some of it on the floor.

The barkeep leans over. "You can't have that dog in here barking and growling at everyone. Take him outside."

I stand and head toward the door, taking my glass with.

"No drinks outside."

I tip the glass back and down the whole thing, spilling a large portion of it down the front of my shirt. I hold up the glass to show the barkeep it's empty and toss it over my shoulder. It smashes onto the floor. The dog grabs my hand and guides me out through the exit.

Once outside, I look down and see the black dog leading me away from the bar. "I said, dog, I know you."

"Yes, you drunken idiot. I know you too."

I reach my hands up to rub my face. "You can talk and I understand you?"

"Geez, I didn't think I left you alone for that long. You are completely blitzed."

"I'm going to need to rest. My legs are buzzing." I sit down in gravel parking lot. My hands pick and dig through the dirt.

Malakai nudges my pocket with his nose. "You're buzzing because your phone is ringing."

I reach into my pocket and pull out my phone. I squint to see I have four missed calls, two from Ginger and two from Nancy. "The women are fighting over me. They all want a piece of this." I belch.

"The way you smell and look right now, yeah, I'm sure that's it. Shouldn't you listen to your messages?"

"Nah. Women just complicate things. From now on, it's just me and this pillow." I scrape together a mound of dirt and rocks and lie down.

Malakai drags me by my t-shirt. "Will you get up? Stop playing games here."

A warm sensation overcomes me and I feel relaxed. My eyes grow heavy and I slowly blink them open, fighting the urge to pass out. "I have to take a leak. We'll move as soon as I find my legs."

"Too late." Malakai paws at the soaked jeans. "You already pissed yourself. You know, you are a piece of work. I'm not sure why I put up with you."

I shrug. My arms are heavy and my legs are numb. I can't bring myself to sit up, let alone stand. As I drift off into a drunken passed out stupor, my mind races. What I want to forget most is now at the front of my mind. I think of my last day on earth as Dr. Scott Weaver.

A wet tongue massages my face and I roll over to my back. Gravel digs into my flesh and I realize I'm still laying in the middle of the street.

"Good. You're awake. I was afraid if you stayed asleep too much longer the shades would get you. Now, get up and follow me."

I sit up and rub the sleep from my eyes. It's still the middle of the night. I reach into my pocket and pull out my phone. "I'm going to call Nancy back."

"Do you really think that is a good idea?"

I shrug but my fingers are already hitting the redial button. My body shakes and shivers and I hiccup into the phone as it rings. My world isn't spinning as much but I still stumble when I rise to my feet. I stagger after Malakai as I wait for someone to pick up. Eventually, her recorded message kicks on and I leave a voicemail.

"Nancy, It's Scott from the diner. You know, I'll have the special? Listen, break up with your boyfriend. I know. I know. I know. Cuz when I find him, I'm going to kill him and then he'll be dead. Cuz I'm dead. So, break up with him." I hang up the phone.

"Are you satisfied?"

I nod and follow Malakai a few more blocks. I stumble and fall a few times. No one is around to take notice. We pass by a liquor store that is just closing up. I try the door. The open sign has been flipped to close but the door isn't locked yet. Jackpot.

"Where are you going now?"

I push through the door and the store clerk is cashing out his drawer. "Hey, buddy. Can't you read the sign? We're closed."

I mumble something I hope is coherent but the man doesn't seem to speak inebriated. I walk right up to him and throw whatever cash I have left on the counter and point to the largest bottle of Maker's Mark whiskey he has. The wax seal makes me feel sophisticated. I'm swaying back and forth, my body jerking with hiccups. I'm still wearing my t-shirt full of holes. He gives me the once over and decides that I need it and slides the bottle my way. I salute him and wander out of the store.

I remain conscious enough to keep going. My mind keeps drifting to see Barry laying in the street as I wander aimlessly behind. Finally, we make it back to my apartment. I fumble with the knob and open the door that's always unlocked. My rule has always been if anyone is desperate enough to break in, then they need whatever they steal more than I do.

I stumble in and search for a clean glass. There are none. I hold the bottle between both hands and gnaw at the seal with my teeth, spitting wax onto the floor. The warm, smooth liquid fills my throat, heating up my whole body.

"Woah there. Slow down. What's your rush?"

I look straight at Malakai and tip the bottle back again, downing several more large gulps.

"Fine. Sorry, I said anything. Do what you want. Just stay in the apartment."

I tip the bottle back again. My head feels like it's drowning. I collapse onto the couch. Maybe I'll just lay here for a few minutes until the room calms down. I stare at a double set of blurred hands and laugh. I can't tell which are truly mine; the ones that heal or the ones that killed a man. My heavy eyelids open and close, slower and slower until it's not worth the effort to keep my eyes open. I close them just for a second…

Chapter 29

There's a constant ringing in my ear and my head vibrates. I open my eyes and realize I'm lying on my phone and someone has been calling me nonstop. I roll up to a sitting position and stare at the phone. Two missed calls from Ginger and five missed calls from Nancy. I smack my lips. My throat is dry and my mouth tastes like I've been sucking on burnt leather straps all night.

The closest sink calls to me. I dunk my head under the kitchen faucet and drink my fill. My stomach rumbles and sloshes with water. I stumble out into the living room, kicking over a mostly empty bottle of Maker's Mark. Damn. Can't believe it wasn't finished. I walk over to the single window in the apartment to take a piss and look out. It's still dark but I feel like I've been asleep for hours.

Malakai's passed out on his back with his feet propped up against the wall. I think about waking him but instead lay back down on the couch. I grab my phone and notice the time. It's 10 pm the following evening. Shit. That means I slept the day away. Less than two hours are left in my sentence.

I look over at Malakai. "Why didn't you wake me?"

Malakai sits up and yawns a full toothy yawn. "I tried but you wouldn't move."

"I should be with Ginger or out working. Something other than lying around here."

The phone rings again. "Why does Nancy keep calling me?"

"You did leave a drunken message on her phone last night. It might have something to do with that."

I pick up one of the tennis balls Malakai has acquired on our patrols, open the window, throw it out, and say, "Fetch."

Malakai moves in that direction and then stops. "That's cold man."

I answer the phone. This is my last shot at protecting Layla. "Oh, Scott. Thank god you finally answered." She cries into the phone.

"Nancy? Calm down. I can barely understand you."

"You were right. You were right about it all." She continues to sob.

"Where you are?"

"Outside the diner. In the back. I should have listened to you."

"I'm coming. Just stay there. Is he there with you?"

"Yes."

"Good. Keep him there. I'm leaving now."

"Hurry Scott."

I grab my jacket and throw it on. "Come on, Malakai. Let's go catch a predator."

Strong wind swirls and the clouds roll in. Thunder rumbles and shakes the earth as we turn the corner and head the two blocks to Angelina's Café. A few fat raindrops fall from the sky and smack me in the face. The clouds above look as if the whole sky is about to come falling down any second. Perfect weather for a showdown.

We get to the front of the café and the lights are out. The last guests have left and the place is closed. I try the front door and it's locked. Malakai rounds the building. I follow him.

Nancy is standing with her arms outstretched, a gun in her hand, pointed directly at a man sitting in the streets. He's hunched over and his hands are holding his side. He starts to push himself backward. Nancy cocks the pistol. "I said, don't move Jeff. Don't make me shoot you again. I'll do it."

He stops moving away and holds his hands up. "You're making a big mistake, you little bitch. No one will believe you. You're just a poor crazy waitress that I took pity on. You were good for publicity."

"You molested my daughter, you son of a bitch." Nancy's hand is shaking and tears stream down her face. If I don't get the gun away from her soon, she's going to kill the man herself. I can't let her throw her life away. Plus, I want that privilege.

"Nancy, I'm here." I walk up behind her and place my hand on her shoulder. My hand slides down her arm until I'm touching the gun with her. "Just give me the gun. You don't want to kill him. You can't take care of Layla if you're locked up behind bars."

"Yeah, Nancy. Listen to the homeless man. He knows what he's talking about."

"You shut the fuck up. I pay rent for a shitty apartment, thank you very much."

My attention is redirected back to Nancy. I touch her shoulder with one hand. My other hand slides further down the barrel of the gun. "Let go of the gun, Nancy. I'll take care of this."

Her hand relaxes and I take the gun from her. She spins around and throws herself into me, sobbing into my chest. The sky lets out another deep rumble and the rain comes pouring down. "Oh Scott, if at any point you think I'm going to lose Layla, promise me you'll kill him."

I hold her in my arms and cradle the back of her head. I whisper into her ear. "Shhh, It's okay now. I got you. You did good." As I'm holding her my right-hand glows. The heat escape from it, causing the light to soothe her.

The mayor watches us. He shouts at me over the rain. "Hey, I know you. You're that guy that's been healing the poor people of the city. You're the one that helped me the night I was mugged. This is just great. You can fix up my wound here and as long as everyone agrees to keep their mouths shut, I won't say anything about our little misunderstanding here."

I release Nancy and step toward the mayor. My hair is soaked and the rain drips off into my eyes. I wipe it away to clear my vision. "Malakai, come wait with Nancy."

Malakai trots over to her and guides her under the awning and out of the rain. I approach the mayor. It looks like the bullet wound is low enough and off to the side that it hasn't done any major damage. He may still need surgery if the bullet didn't go all the way through, but unfortunately, he'll live. I'm close enough for my hand to have a response. It stays dark and cold.

"Do the right thing here and I'll make sure my people take good care of you. You want money? How about a building named after you? Whatever you want, I can give it to you. I practically own this city."

I can feel my hands start to shake. My face feels hot as I squeeze the handle of the gun still in my other hand.

He lifts his shirt and points to the wound. "It's just right here. Do your thing."

If there is the slightest bit of truth behind what Layla said, there is no way my light will give me a flicker. Even fellow prison inmates don't forgive child molesters. That's an automatic shanking. I hover my free hand over the wound and kneel next to him, keeping the gun in plain view.

"That smell." Malakai sniffs the wind. He leaves Nancy and tracks over to us. He bends over the mayor and snorts. "The syringe. Scott, it's the same smell that was on the syringe."

"You said I could have anything, right?"

"Yes, anything. Just stop fooling around. I'm bleeding here."

I look down and see the steady swirl of blood flowing from his wound, mixing with the rain, and flowing away from him toward the closest drainage pipe. The shades will soon smell the blood and come hunting for him. I press my hand into his side. He grunts and sucks in air from the pressure over the wound.

"I want my sweet, soulful, percussion playing lunatic back."

"Who?"

"I want my Barry. I hired him to follow you around when you were making your daily visits to the hospital. He told me some interesting things about you and a poor sick girl. He even filmed it. But you already knew that since you were the one who removed the camera from the bear."

"You don't have proof of anything. I destroyed the camera right before I had that homeless man removed from the hospital. My security detail did some digging when I saw him following me. They informed me of his little habit. It's amazing how quickly an addict will keep his mouth shut if you give him what he's been resisting for so long."

I grab hold of his neck and squeeze. His mouth gapes open and his eyes bulge like a fish choking on air. I slam his head down onto the ground.

Malakai pulls on my pants. "Scott, he's not worth it. Think about it. You are so close to getting out of here. Don't let this scum ruin it for you. There's still a few minutes left. If we leave now, we may be able to find you one last heal."

I turn my head and look at Nancy watching from a distance. Her hands are folded and I can't tell if she's praying or pleading with me. I turn back toward the mayor and release my grip. I give him one more shove for good measure and slowly rise to my feet.

"I'll have you locked in jail for assaulting the mayor."

Jail would be a welcome vacation from the hell I'm in now. Fat droplets of water smack the ground and bounce back into the air. I switch the gun back to my right hand and turn back toward the mayor. Out from the sewers rises a single black shade, this one larger than any I have ever seen and more dense, so thick I could touch it. It rolls and twists onto itself. Its shape, more human than any before it, follows the blood path leading right for us.

I look the mayor dead in the face. "I want Layla to have her innocence back."

"I have been nothing but nice to that little girl. I loved her as if she were my own."

"You fucking molested her."

"Is that what she told you? Kids have a tendency to exaggerate things."

"She's only seven. She's just a little girl. What you did…I pray for your sake that she was exaggerating ." I raise the gun, cock it, and point it directly at the mayor's head. The shade floats closer, now only a few feet away from the mayor's head. It rises straight into the air and splits down the middle, forming into two separate large shadowed hands. One drifts toward the mayor while the other hand reaches for me.

I hear Malakai in the background. "Scott, please. Killing him means eternal damnation. There's no backing out of that. This is your soul. Put the gun down and walk away. The shade will deal with him."

The rain muffles all other sounds of the city. The shade's hand floats in front of me and I feel a sense of calm. It beckons me forward, its finger signaling me to lean closer. The other hand hovers over the mayor's throat like it's waiting for me to choose. If I use my light right now, I can scare the shade off.

I won't be able to heal the mayor, but I could take him to the hospital again. That might give me my last heal as a technicality. Then again, that would leave this man alive to molest again.

Malakai doesn't understand. I'm already damned to hell. No one receives redemption from killing themselves. Suicide is too great of a sin to come back from. I made a choice in my last lifetime. I chose to end it then and I choose to end it now. The only thing left to atone for is what I did to this woman and her child.

"You're wrong, Malakai. It has to be me."

Chapter 30

I feel like I'm spinning and being sucked into a vortex. I hear a loud 'Pop'. Light surrounds me from all directions. My body is warm and dry. My arms are completely smooth. Not a single scar marks my body. I'm flawless, glowing, and I feel fantastic. If this is hell, then I'm going to like it here.

I'm standing in a completely bare room. All the walls are white and reflect light, making me squint. There are two doors at each end of the room, one to my right and one to my left. I turn left and walk toward that door first. My feet seem to glide across the room. There's a certain peace that fills me as if I finally understand everything and have everything I'm ever wanted. I'm a little disappointed with the lack of lava pits, rivers of fire, and demons with pitchforks poking the locals, but I guess this version of hell is alright. There's a small envelope taped to the door with my name on it. I grab it and rip it open. Inside is a small note…

Dear Scott,

You have finally proven yourself worthy and demonstrated that you can once again put others before yourself. All your past sins are forgiven. Thank you for your service.

The door in front of you leads back should you need to tie up any loose ends. Feel free to see who you want, but I will give you only 24 hours. After that time, you will be transported back to this room and then you will move on through the other door.

Congratulations for surviving purgatory. Enjoy your last 24 hours and welcome to your afterlife.

Sincerely,

'The Big Man'

Woah. Only 24 hours. I'm going to want to spend at least 23 of those with a certain member of the stripping group. I better get to it. I reach my hand out and turn the knob of the door…

Chapter 31

It's one of those mornings when you can just tell it's going to be perfect outside. The crystal blue of the sky is not even marked by a single cloud. Outside of Angelina's Café and the smell of fatty bacon, salty eggs, sweet maple syrup, and cheesy biscuits fills my nostrils. My stomach rumbles something fierce. I'm so hungry I'm going to scarf up my food like a dog would until I puke and then I may just eat the vomit too.

The doorbell chimes my entrance. The walls are back to their pea shit shade of green paint. The counters are still clean and the seats are still intact, but with the time that will change. Blonde pigtails come around the corner, skipping toward me.

"I knew you'd be back. I told Mom to leave your seat open."

I follow her toward my corner booth. "I love what you've done with the place. It's starting to look familiar again."

"Yeah. After Mom broke up with Jeff and he disappeared, she wanted to change some things around. She said we'd honor you and change it back to the way you liked it."

I slide into my seat and pat next to me. "Do you want to sit down?"

"No, thanks. I'm working today. Mom says it teaches me responsibilities. But I know someone who will want to see you. I'll go get him."

I hear a whining from the back and Malakai sprints through the café heading directly toward me. Tied into his fur on his head are two small hot pink bows. He leaps up into my lap I ruffle his fur. "Oh, who's a good boy?"

He drowns me with kisses. "Did you miss me you big fluffy thing you?"

I break down. I pet Malakai over and over as every customer in the restaurant is treated to an awkward scene of a grown man crying over a dog.

"What the hell happened? I saw the shade enter you. The gun went off and you were just gone."

"Are you crazy, not in front of the girl"

"The kid knows everything. She can understand me. It's been two weeks since you left. How else was I going to get pizza crust from Canyon?" He sniffs my arms. "Where are all your scars? And what is this scent you have on you? You smell…clean?"

I smile. "Turns out you were a good guide after all."

"But then what are you doing back here?"

"The 'Big Man' gave me 24 hours to settle things. Figured I had to check on my best friend and have one last amazing meal together. I also probably owe both Nancy and Ginger an explanation."

He gives me one more big wet kiss. "Nancy is okay. Now that Layla can understand me, she's been trying to explain things to her mom. It's a process but I think it will help when she sees you."

"So, you'll be alright without me then?"

"Of course. I told you, I'm my own dog. Plus, Layla needs me now. I've been reassigned. Life is a little less punchy, but the food is incredible."

"I feel like I left you down. I never took you to see the ocean or learned how to brush your hair." I point to the bows.

"Real men wear pink."

Nancy walks toward me with a big plate of food and a cup filled with coffee. She sets the mound in front of me. She smiles and slaps my shoulder. This time I don't flinch. "Layla told me you were here so I thought you needed something extra today." She reaches over to one of the other tables and grabs a bottle of hot sauce for me.

I pick up a fork and poke at the food. It smells delicious but I can't even begin to make out what it is. "It looks…interesting?"

"I'm calling it, 'The Blister City Hasher'. It's going to be a permanent menu item. Sweet potato hash and black beans, covered in ground pork and eggs severed frittata style, all smothered in cheddar cheese, topped with green onion and salsa verde. Oh, and with a side of bacon and a biscuit for our favorite customers." She winks.

I shrug and take a forkful of the food. It is a blend of flavors that mix and makes my taste buds sing. The sweet of the potato and the salt of the pork with just a hint of heat blends perfectly with the savoriness of the cheese. There's not even the slightest hint of char. It is the best thing I've ever tasted. "This is too good, Nancy. Did you guys hire a new chef?"

"Yep. The last one started too many kitchen fires. This new one's kind of cute too. I think we'll keep him around."

I continue to shovel my food in. "I'm not going to be coming around here anymore and I wanted to make sure you and Layla were taken care of before I left."

"Things are good. After you left, the police found some photos on the mayor's cell phone. They searched his place and found video footage of other kids. They're saying the victims are going to sue his estate. All that money can help begin the healing process for all those poor kids and get all his money to aid in the healing process."

I finish my plate and spend the rest of the morning laughing with Malakai and Layla as we relay some of our adventures together. Nancy stops by in between her tables to listen. I almost think about telling them the truth of who I really am and what I did to their family all those years ago. Nancy looks completely happy; almost at peace. Digging up old wounds by telling the truth is not going to help them move on so I remain quiet. I still have a few things left to do, so I say goodbye. We share a few hugs and I thank them before I head out the door.

Malakai follows me to the door and I reach down to pet him. "So, do you want me to hug you or what?"

"What, and create another embarrassing scene for you?"

"Whatever." I pull him in and give him one big hug. "Thanks for taking care of my drunk ass and setting me on the right path. You're a good dog." I ruffle his head and scratch behind his ears.

"No more binges between now and when you move on. I have to take care of Layla now and I can't be expected to babysit you."

I give him one more good scratch and head through the door. I think I'm actually going to miss that fur ball. The sun is still shining brightly in the sky. It's warm but not sweltering hot, just completely comfortable. I take my jacket off and walk in just a short-sleeved shirt with jeans. My typical gray shirt with holes has been replaced by a white t-shirt. Even my jacket is missing its normal blood stains and bullet holes.

I decide to take a stroll along my patrol area one last time. I travel up and down Graham and Sugar Creek. I pass The Underground where I spent too many nights wasted. I pass the strip joint where I spent too many nights and too much money on lap dances. The city looks different in the daylight, brighter, cleaner. Bars still line all the Family Dollar Stores and there are still a lot of thugs lurking in the shadows, waiting for nightfall.

But that's not my concern anymore. That's for the next sorry bastard who finds himself stuck in purgatory.

After I've hit every last highlight on my walk, I find myself standing outside of a pale blue townhouse with a white door. I knock on the door. Two weeks with no word from me. She's going to be pissed.

No answer so I knock one more time. The door clicks as it's being unlocked from the other side. I flinch as Ginger opens the door, anticipating a slap or something worse. The expression on her face is blank and I can't tell if she's pissed at me or not. "Before you say anything, let me explain."

She folds her arms. "Two weeks? And not even a text? Oh, this better be good."

I reach my hand up and rub the back of my neck. "Well, I had just found out that Barry died and I was out blowing off steam. I may have taken that too far. Then Malakai shows up and we…"

She reaches out and pulls me into her, planting her lips on mine to shut me up.

I pull back. "So, you're not mad?"

"Mad? I'm a little upset, yes but not mad. I'm assuming that since your skin is smooth and missing its iconic scar pattern that you finally reached your quota and are here to say goodbye. I never had sex with an angel before."

"After what I'm going to do to you, I won't be allowed angelhood. Plus, I never looked good in white."

"Well, how much time do we have?"

"About 18 hours. Give or take a few minutes."

"Then you better get in here and take your clothes off. I want to give you a proper send off with one last dance."

Good thing I exchanged my last paycheck for a giant wad of singles. I follow her into the house and close the door behind me.

About the Author

Brooke Reynolds is a writer from Charlotte, North Carolina. She is known for writing short stories typically in the horror, neo-noir, or transgressive satire genre. HEALERS is her first novel.

Reynolds graduated from the Pennsylvania State University with a Bachelor of Sciences. She received her DVM from The Virginia-Maryland Regional College of Veterinary Medicine. She currently practices small animal medicine with a special interest in surgery and dentistry.

She has had numerous short stories published online and in print in various markets such as The Scarlet Leaf Review, The Airgonaut, Massacre Magazine, Fantasia Divinity, The Literary Hatchet, Ghost Parachute, Riggwelter Magazine, Defenestration, Adelaide, Every Day Fiction, Ricky's Back Yard, Coffin Bell, Ink Stains, and Sanitarium Magazine.

Her story "Dr. Google" won 2nd place in the 2016 Short Story Contest for Channillo and her story "Bang Bang" received runner up in the 2018 Flash Suite Contest at Defenestrationism. She was also named a finalist for both the 2018 and 2019 Adelaide Literary Award for Best Short Story.

She lives with her husband and two children.

You can follow her on twitter @psubamit or check out her website reynoldswrites.org

www.ingramcontent.com/pod-product-compliance
Lightning Source LLC
Chambersburg PA
CBHW021144190726

48288CB00008B/2817